Whack The Mole
Lucy McGuffin, Psychic Amateur Detective Book 2

Maggie March

Chihuahua Publishing

Contents

Chapter One

THE THING ABOUT BEING a human lie detector is that people will surprise you with the strangest fabrications at the oddest times. Take right now. Rusty Newton, one of Whispering Bay's finest is looking me straight in the eye, and he's just told me a whopper.

I shift my weight from foot to foot. I've been standing behind this counter for over three hours without a break. It's the busiest morning we've had all week. And it's been a record-breaking week here at The Bistro by the Beach, the café I co-own along with my friend, Sarah Powers. Probably because I've become a bit of a celebrity. A small-town celebrity to be sure, but when you're responsible for nabbing one of America's most sought-after serial killers, people want to come and gawk at you.

Not that I mind the gawking. It's been terrific for business.

"You want how many muffins again?" I ask Rusty.

"A dozen." He pulls a piece of paper from the front pocket of his uniform shirt. Rusty Newton is in his mid-forties and has been a cop here in town forever. He's super sweet, but not the brightest bulb on the force. "And five lattes, four turkey sandwiches, a tub of Sarah's mac and cheese and six oatmeal raisin cookies."

"And this is for the crew back at the police station?"

"Who else would I be getting such a big order for?"

Not for the Whispering Bay police department, that's for sure. For one thing, Zeke Grant, the chief of police, has already been in this morning for his coffee and muffin fix. And Cindy, the department's receptionist, is on a diet. She hasn't caught so much as a whiff of one of my muffins in weeks.

But that's not what gave Rusty away.

It's the little hairs on the back of my neck. Whenever I hear a lie, they automatically start to tingle.

Being able to sniff out lies is a gift I've had ever since I was old enough to tell a lie myself. A gift I never appreciated until a few days ago when it helped me solve the murder of Abby Delgado, a prominent member of the Sunshine Ghost Society, a local club that claims to commune with the dead. But that's another story.

I punch Rusty's order into the computer. "Is this all to go?"

Before he can answer, another one of Whispering Bay's finest comes up to the counter. Officer Travis Fontaine is the newest member of the force, and he looks almost as yummy as one of my double chocolate chip muffins. I wish I could say it was the uniform, but it's not.

Travis is six foot three with dark blond hair and fierce green eyes. He spent eight years on the Dallas police force before recently moving here to live near his dad, a retired homicide detective, all of which makes Travis a good son.

He's also arrogant, and the easiest person I've ever read in my life. Not because his face gives anything away. On the contrary. Travis has a poker face that could make him a bundle in Vegas. It's just that for some reason where he's concerned my Spidey sense is on ultra-alert.

"Rusty just put in a quite an order," I say. "Is the police department having a party?"

Travis doesn't so much as twitch. "No party. Just a bunch of hungry cops."

Right.

I have to admit, this charade of theirs has me intrigued. What do they want with all this food?

"It'll take a few minutes to get that order together."

"No problem." Travis leans into the counter. "How's your head?"

"Still sore, but I'll live, thanks."

My head met up with the backside of a frying pan a few days ago. I still shudder whenever I think about how close I came to becoming the Angel of Death's latest victim. Good thing my dog Paco was there to save me.

Speaking of Paco, he has his own unique form of Spidey sense because he runs up to me like he knows I'm thinking about him. "Hey, little guy!"

I inherited the adorable little mutt when I solved the murder of his former owner Susan Van Dyke. His name used to be Cornelius, but that was way too stuffy, so he's Paco now. The members of the Sunshine Ghost Society think he's a ghost whisperer. Which, of course, is silly, but like I said, he's special. It's almost like he can understand what the humans around him are saying.

I'm allergic to dogs with fur, but after all we've been through there's no way I'm giving him up, so I'm on medication to keep from itching. It's not supposed to make me drowsy, but it still does sometimes. I consider it a small price to pay for keeping him. I live in the apartment above the café, and Paco spends his days going up and down the stairs between our home and The Bistro's dining area. The customers love his cute antics, and Sarah finds him adorable as well.

Paco runs around to the other side of the counter to greet Travis. "Hey, boy." Travis squats down to scratch him behind the ears.

According to Lanie Miller, the manager of the Whispering Bay Animal Shelter, Travis is on the lookout for a dog. I try to imagine what breed would go best with his personality. Probably a rottweiler. Or a pit bull.

Travis rises to his full height and gives Rusty a side look that makes the older cop slink away. It also makes me nervous. I haven't known Travis long, but like I said, I have a pretty good read on him. He hasn't asked me out yet, but I have a sinking feeling that's about to change.

"Are you busy Friday night?"

Oh boy. I've been expecting this ever since Travis told me that he's now become a "muffin man." To most people that wouldn't mean a thing, but besides my lie detecting skills, I also make the best muffins in Whispering Bay. Not that I would say that. But everyone else does, so who am I to argue with them?

"Friday night is when Will and I watch *America's Most Vicious Criminals*."

Will Cunningham is my best friend. I've been secretly in love with him ever since my seventh birthday party when he saved me from a pack of rabid squirrels. We started our Friday night TV and pizza tradition when I moved back to town after graduating from culinary school, and I wouldn't miss it for anything in the world.

Since moving to town, Travis and Will have become friends too. They even play in the same basketball league. If Travis suspects that I have feelings for Will, he doesn't let on. "So how about tonight then?"

"How about tonight what?" I hate playing dumb, but I have no experience when it comes to fending guys off.

"How about we grab something to eat?"

"Tonight's my book club."

He spears me with a look that makes me squirm. "I guess that's better than telling me you have to wash your hair."

"No really. I got invited to Betty Jean's book club, and I promised to bring muffins. Apparently, there's a big waiting list to join so I didn't dare refuse."

Betty Jean Collins is a regular customer here at The Bistro and a real character. She's a prominent member of the Gray Flamingos, a local senior citizens activist group. She's also the eighty-year-old female equivalent of a hound dog. No man under the age of sixty is safe from her.

At the mention of Betty Jean, Travis breaks down and grins. When he smiles like that, his eyes become even greener. He really is quite attractive. But he knows it, so that spoils it a little.

"So you're busy tonight and tomorrow. How about Saturday night?"

This guy doesn't give up, does he? I try my hardest to think of a reason to turn him down. But there isn't one.

"I could maybe possibly be free Saturday night."

Did I really just say that?

"What would it take to make that a definitely free?"

I'm about to answer when—"Lucy!" Travis and I whip around to see Brittany Kelly rush into the café.

Brittany Kelly and I have a weird history. We both grew up in Whispering Bay and attended school together. Our relationship, however, got off on the wrong foot way back in kindergarten when she lied about stealing a brand-new set of paintbrushes. Being a naïve five-year-old, I told the teacher about Brittany's lie which got me labeled as a tattletale and earned me Brittany's disdain for the next twelve years.

At least, that's how I saw the situation.

Brittany viewed things differently. Apparently, all this time she's wanted to be my friend. At least that's what she says now. She works for the Whispering Bay Chamber of Commerce (a job her rich daddy helped her nab) and came up with our city's tagline, *Whispering Bay, the safest city in America*!

Brittany spots Travis, and her brown eyes go wide. I have brown eyes too, but Brittany's have an extra oomph to them.

"Hello, Travis." Her voice sounds breathy and strangely seductive. How does she do that?

"Hello, Brittany." Travis smiles down at her, but it's a more patient smile than an encouraging one. I admit I'm intrigued that he doesn't seem to be as wowed by Brittany as every other male on the planet.

She wets her bottom lip. "I hope you don't mind, but I need to speak to Lucy. It's super important."

Travis gives me a meaningful look. "We'll finish this conversation later." He politely joins Rusty at the far end of the counter to give us privacy.

"Hey, Brittany, what's up?" I ask like I'm happy to see her. Which, for once, I am. If she hadn't interrupted us, I would have said yes to Travis which would have been a big mistake. According to Cindy, in the short time Travis has been in town women have been showing up at police headquarters in droves hoping to get a chance to speak to him.

I have absolutely no intention of becoming a member of the Travis Fontaine fan club. Plus, if Will finds out I went out with Travis, which he would because nothing in this town stays a secret, it might ruin any chance I have with him.

Am I attracted to Travis? Yes.

Am I interested in any sort of long-term relationship with him? That would be a resounding *no*.

Brittany makes a pained face. "I just spoke to Tara, and she says that the film crew will be here first thing Monday morning. I knew it would be fast, but I'm kind of freaking out here."

"Relax, it will all be fine."

"Fine? This is the Cooking Channel! We only get one chance to impress them. We absolutely have to be picked for their new show."

Battle of the Beach Eats (great name, huh?) is the Cooking Channel's newest hit show. It's a reality TV competition that pits restaurants in the same town against one another until one by one, each restaurant gets eliminated and the last one standing is crowned the winner. Which means if we get selected, The Bistro by the Beach will be competing with the other eateries in Whispering Bay, including The Harbor House, which is owned by Brittany's daddy. The prize money is twenty-five thousand dollars, which I could certainly use.

Tara, the show's producer, is scheduled to come with her film crew to get some local footage. According to Brittany, if they like what they see, then we're a shoo-in.

"No worries," I say. "Sarah and I are planning to come in on Sunday to make sure everything looks spic and span. If Whispering Bay isn't picked to be on *Battle of the Beach Eats*, it won't be The Bistro's fault."

Brittany looks me over like she's my commanding officer and I'm a grunt lining up for inspection. "Good to hear. So, about Paco. Do you think it's a good idea to have him running around the café all day? I mean, I love him to death, but what if Tara gets wigged out by it? Not everyone is a dog person, Lucy."

She did not just go there.

"Paco stays. End of story."

Brittany sighs dramatically. "My intel says that it's down to us and some city named Catfish Cove about a hundred miles east of here. Apparently, they're super environmentally correct so we have to do everything we can to convince Tara that Whispering Bay is the wholesome American beach town they're looking for. I've ordered the city's maintenance department to trim all the trees on Main Street, and I've got wreaths coming in for all the businesses to hang on their front doors, and ... well, I kind of went over budget, so we simply *have* to get picked."

Wreaths for all the businesses? Yikes. I can't imagine how much that might have cost.

"You know, Lucy, we have so much more to talk about. Maybe we can do lunch again?"

Brittany and I had lunch yesterday like regular girlfriends. It wasn't as horrible as I imagined, but I don't want a repeat anytime soon either. "Okay, sure."

She pulls out her planner. "When?"

"Um, maybe after the film crew does their thing? I think we'll both be pretty busy until then."

"Right! You're so smart, Lucy. Call me tomorrow so we can make plans!" She blows me a kiss on her way out.

I slump against the counter. Talking to Brittany for five minutes is almost as exhausting as spending the morning serving customers.

Sarah comes out from the kitchen and hands me two big bags. "Funny, I don't remember the police department ever placing such a large order."

Neither do I.

Rusty pays in cash, then he and Travis take the bags and leave.

"Whew," says Sarah. "I'm glad things are slowing down some. Want to take a breather? You haven't sat down all morning."

Through the glass pane window, I watch Rusty and Travis get into their squad car and my Spidey sense slaps me up the side of the head. Or maybe its residual ache from the frying pan incident. Whatever.

But something tells me to follow them, and if I've learned anything in the past week, it's that I need to listen to myself.

"Do you mind if I take an early lunch break?"

"No problem. Jill and I can handle things for a bit."

"Thanks!" I grab a sweater and Paco's leash. He happily jumps into the passenger seat of my VW beetle.

Since Travis and Rusty are in a squad car, it's not hard to spot them.

I stay in the right-hand lane, three cars behind, going slow but not too slow because I want to keep up.

The Whispering Bay police station is next door to city hall, but instead of turning into the parking lot, Travis keeps on driving.

I knew they were up to something!

Paco sticks his head out the window. "Get back in," I urge in case either Travis or Rusty are looking. The last thing I want is for one of them to spot me.

The squad car takes a right into Dolphin Isles, a new residential community of cookie-cutter homes. Whispering Bay is a coastal town of about ten thousand year-long residents, mostly young families, and retirees. But there's also a substantial vacation and snowbird crowd that rent homes in this subdivision.

Travis parks the squad car on the side of the road. I stay half a block down shielding my car behind a big palm tree. I'm confident they can't see me.

Paco barks like he wants to ask a question.

"Shhh," I warn. "We're trying to stay incognito."

He freezes like he understands, which is actually pretty cute.

I glance back at the squad car, expecting Travis or Rusty or both of them to get out, but nothing happens.

Could they be on a stakeout?

My heart speeds up at the thought. But that makes no sense. All that food for just the two of them?

I make a mental note to buy myself a pair of binoculars when I notice a jogger coming toward them. Male, mid-thirties, lean build, navy blue hoodie. He slows down and approaches the squad car. Travis hands him the two bags of food through the car window, then the man takes off jogging in the opposite direction.

After a couple of minutes, Travis and Rusty drive away.

I make sure they're gone, then I follow the jogger.

Chapter Two

I'VE NEVER FOLLOWED ANYONE before, but it's actually kind of fun. No wonder Harriet (Harriet the Spy was one of my favorite movies as a kid) was always writing down observations in that little journal of hers. Besides the binoculars, I should also probably pick up a couple of notebooks. Just in case.

The jogger goes up three streets and into a one-story stucco home on the edge of a cul-de-sac. The garage door is closed, and the driveway is empty.

"What do you think that was about?" I ask Paco.

He turns his head the way dogs do in that quizzical manner that looks so adorable.

Since I'm not as prepared as Harriet, I scribble down the address on the back of a Tiny's pizza coupon and slip it into my tote. After a couple of minutes of nothing happening, I drive back to The Bistro.

What did I just witness?

On the surface, it all looks pretty benign. Except Rusty lied about the food (which I already knew).

But why?

Who is this mysterious jogger?

And why the sneaky food handoff?

The rest of the work day goes by quickly. The Bistro stops serving food at two p.m. and luckily, Sarah has clean-up duty today because tonight is my first book club meeting and with everything that's happened in the past week, I haven't had time to read the book.

Confession: I don't even have a copy of the book.

Since Betty Jean has already warned me that she can always tell when someone is fudging it, I need to take care of this situation ASAP. The last thing I want is to be kicked out of the book club on my first night.

I download J.W. Quicksilver's newest espionage thriller onto my Kindle. Book club starts in less than five hours so I won't have time to finish it, but I figure that if I skip right to all the big scenes (that would be the ones involving either death or sex), no one will be the wiser.

When Betty Jean first invited me to her book club, I made excuses not to join. I'm the only member who isn't eligible for the AARP, but when you're facing death in the form of a frying pan to the head, your life flashes before you in ways you've never imagined. I need to work on becoming a better person. Which means trying new things.

I read for an hour straight before I get up and stretch. Betty Jean was right. This stuff is ridiculously addicting. Too many explosions and assassinations for my taste, but the sex scenes have totally managed to grab my attention. I mean, do people really *do* this stuff? They must, or someone wouldn't have written it, right?

I grab my laptop and google this mysterious J.W. Quicksilver which is as about as phony a pen name as you can get. The bio on his website shows a picture of an old-fashioned typewriter instead of an author photo which means that not only is J.W. not using his real name, he doesn't want anyone to know who he is.

Betty Jean thinks he uses a pen name because he has a top-secret government job which would explain why he knows so much about the spy business. But I think it's because of the sex scenes. I'd bet my apple walnut cream cheese muffin recipe that J.W. is a bald, middle-aged schoolteacher living in the Bible belt with a wife and six kids.

His books have won awards and his latest, our book club selection, *Assassin's Honor*, has been on the best seller list for over a month now.

I wonder what J.W. would think about blue hoodie guy? Who is he? And why does he need so much food?

I fish out the Tiny's pizza coupon from my sweater pocket and type the address in my computer. It comes up on a list of vacation rentals and the broker for the listing is Kitty Pappas. Kitty is a total sweetheart and Whispering Bay royalty. She's a founding member of the Bunco Babes, a local group that plays Bunco once a week. Everyone in town knows her and her husband Steve.

I give her a call.

"Hey, Kitty, it's Lucy McGuffin."

"Lucy! I've been thinking of you!" Kitty wants to know all about my near-death experience at the hands of a crazy sociopath. I can't blame her since nothing like that has ever happened in Whispering Bay before, but I'm getting tired of telling the same story over and over. Roger Van Cleave, who co-owns the Whispering Bay Gazette, has been after me for an interview. I think I'll take him up on it. That way I can just refer people to the article.

After I give Kitty enough details to satisfy her, I ask her about the property in Dolphin Isles.

"Are you looking for a place to rent? I thought you loved living over The Bistro."

"Oh, it's not for me. It's for a ... friend."

"I'll be happy to give your friend the information on the house. Currently, it's leased out, but it's a short-term rental. Just till the end of the month."

"Oh, really," I say trying to sound casual. "A snowbird?"

"Hardly. The couple who rented the place are in their thirties. Honeymooners, I think. I can't show you the house since it's occupied, but if you give me your friend's email address, I can send them pictures and any information they might need."

"Oh, um, thanks. I don't have her email address on me, but I'll pass the info along."

Yikes. After solving the mystery behind Abby Delgado's death, I promised myself I wouldn't lie anymore. But here I am, doing just that.

We say our goodbyes. After Kitty's phone call I'm more confused than ever. Why on earth are Rusty and Travis getting food for a couple of honeymooners?

"Mommy is going out for a while," I tell Paco, who's laid out on the couch (because being The Bistro's mascot is apparently hard work). "Be a good boy."

He yawns and goes back to sleep.

The library doesn't close for a couple of hours, so I still have time to swing by before book club starts at seven.

Since Will is the head librarian and I'm his best friend, everyone at the library knows me. Sally Reynolds, one of newer media specialists, waves to me from the reference desk. She's from somewhere down in south Florida, and since moving to town a couple of weeks ago, she's come to The Bistro at least three times to get one of my muffins, which means Sally has excellent taste.

"Hey, Lucy! Will is in his office."

I stop by her desk to admire her new hair color. Sally switches hair color the way I change T-shirts. Today, her chin-length hair is bright pink. A look she can totally rock because she has that kind of face. She's wearing a black sweatshirt with the words WINTER IS COMING. Besides a love of muffins, we have a couple of other things in common.

We both like wearing shirts with quirky sayings, and we're both huge *Game of Thrones* fans.

"Nice," she says pointing to my YOU AIN'T SEEN MUFFIN YET T-shirt.

"Thanks. Say, have you ever heard of an author named J.W. Quicksilver?"

"I'm a librarian, Lucy. Of course I've heard of him."

"Funny, because when I mentioned him to Will last week, he seemed clueless."

Sally rolls her eyes. "Will's a great guy, but he's a bit of a book snob."

Tell me about it. Will's preference for the classics over popular fiction is well known. I'm surprised that he stoops low enough to watch *America's Most Vicious Criminals*.

"You wouldn't happen to have a copy of his latest book, *Assassin's Honor*? I'm supposed to read it for Betty Jean's book club."

"Betty Jean Collins?" Sally playfully shivers. "I might be new to town, but that's a name that makes me want to hide behind my desk. She comes in every morning demanding to know if we've gotten any new books." She tsks. "Total book hog."

"That's her. Do you have a copy of the book?"

"Sorry, it's a new release, so we're all out. We have a waiting list if you want to put your name on it."

"Book club is tonight. But that's okay, I have it on my Kindle."

Sally plugs her ears with her fingers. "La-la-la-la .... Can't hear you!"

I laugh. "Sorry."

"I hate to think that one day there might not be any print books left in the world." She sighs. "So, have you started reading *Assassin's Honor*? What do you think of it?"

"Honestly? It's pretty addicting."

She smiles impishly. "Have you gotten to chapter fourteen yet?"

My cheeks go hot. Betty Jean "warned" me about this chapter already. "I kind of skipped ahead to it."

"Whew!" Sally fans herself with her hand. "That J.W. Quicksilver sure can write a sex scene. It makes you wonder what he's like in real life."

Will pokes his head out his office door. "Lucy. I thought I heard your voice. C'mon in."

Sally and I both startle like we've been caught with our hands in the muffin jar. I head into Will's office where I make myself at home.

Will's office is basically a glorified cubicle with four walls, but it's private and cozy. The walls are covered with pictures of family and friends, including one of Will and my brother Sebastian when they graduated high school. There's also one of me in an apron standing behind the counter on the day that Sarah and I officially became owners of The Bistro. I'm grinning like a fool. Probably because it was one of the happiest days of my life.

"How's your head?" he asks.

"Better."

"Good. I'm glad you came by. Saves me a phone call. I have to cancel tomorrow night."

"Why? What's going on?" Will never cancels our Friday pizza and TV night if he can help it. Especially not when there's a new episode of *America's Most Vicious Criminals*.

"It's work related. Something I can't get out of. Will you record the show? We can watch it later."

"Sure." I get right down to it. "Travis and Rusty came by The Bistro this morning."

"Don't Travis and Rusty come by every morning for their coffee?"

"Yeah, but they ordered a lot of food."

"Where's this going?"

"They said it was for the police department, but that was a lie."

Will sits back in his chair and looks at me. There are only five people in the world who know about my special gift. My parents, my brother Sebastian, Travis's dad (who I told just a few days ago), and Will.

But there's one thing about my lie detecting skills that Will and the others aren't aware of. Will is the only person I know who I've never caught in a lie.

Not because he doesn't lie, because let's face it, everyone lies. But I've never caught Will in any sort of deception. Which is odd, but I figure it's because my feelings for him must somehow get in the way of my Spidey sense.

"So after they left The Bistro, Paco and I kind of followed them and naturally, I was right. The food wasn't for the police."

"*Kind* of followed them?"

"We one hundred percent followed them. But don't worry, they didn't see us. I made sure of that."

Will shakes his head the way he does whenever he disapproves of one of my schemes. "Lucy, what are you up to now?"

I lean forward. "Hear me out. I followed them to Dolphin Isles. They parked their squad car along the side of a road. Then this guy jogged by and Travis handed him the food real sneaky like. Then a couple of minutes later, Travis and Rusty took off and I followed the jogger to a house on a cul-de-sac."

"And?"

"*And*? You don't find that suspicious?"

"Maybe this guy is a friend of theirs."

"I know everyone in town. I've never seen this guy before. Plus, I found out from Kitty Pappas that the house the guy went into is being rented by a couple of honeymooners."

He absorbs this for a few seconds. "The Bistro doesn't deliver. Does it?"

"No, but—"

"A couple on their honeymoon have someone deliver food to them. They sound like a regular Bonnie and Clyde."

"A dozen muffins? Six sandwiches? That doesn't sound like something a couple on their honeymoon orders out."

Will's blue eyes glint with humor. "Maybe they're into kinky food fights."

"So they have the cops delivering them food?"

"Lucy, you can't go around following people and making wild assumptions. I'm sure there's a perfectly logical explanation. Just ask Rusty or Travis what they were doing."

Not the attitude I'm looking for.

I can't very well ask Travis or Rusty what they were doing without giving away that I was following them, and Will knows it.

"Put all that energy you have into something productive. Like making sure everything is ready to go when the Cooking Channel film crew comes on Monday."

"You sound like Brittany."

Speaking of Brittany ... Will has had a crush on Brittany since forever. Last Friday night they finally went out on their first date, but something happened, and the date ended early. Later that night while we were alone in the kitchen, Will was about to tell me something that sounded really promising, but we were interrupted, and we haven't had a chance to talk about it since. "We never got to talk about your big date," I say cautiously.

"Yeah. About that ..." Will readjusts his glasses which is something he does whenever he gets nervous or pensive. "It was okay."

"Just okay?" I try not to sound too gleeful as my mind imagines all the dozens of things that might have gone wrong. Maybe Brittany eats with her mouth full. Will hates that. But ... no. I've seen Brittany eat. She picks at her food like a little bird.

"Brittany and I didn't have a lot to talk about. Except for her job. She's pretty passionate about that."

Aha! It's just as I suspected. They have nothing in common. Which is way better than her eating with her mouth full.

"Are you going to ask her out again?" *Please say no*.

"I don't know. Probably not anytime soon."

"Travis asked me out," I blurt. "On a date."

Will's gaze sharpens. "What did you say?"

"I haven't given him an answer yet. What do you think? Should I go out with him?" I hold my breath while I wait for him to answer. Please tell me that I shouldn't go out with Travis.

"Do you want to go out with him?"

I flop back in my chair. This wishy-washy attitude wasn't what I was expecting. It's like that moment in the kitchen the other night never happened.

"I don't know. He's not my type."

"You have a type?"

Before I can answer, Sally knocks on the open door. "Sorry to interrupt, but you asked me to tell you when the new AV equipment came in?"

Will smiles at her. "Thanks, Sally."

"I need to get going anyway." I rise from my chair. "Don't want to be late for my first book club meeting at Betty Jean's."

"What I wouldn't give to be a fly on the wall."

"You could always join. Betty Jean says the club is full, but I'm sure she'd make an exception for you," I tease. "We're dissecting J.W. Quicksilver's newest thriller. Lots of big action and hot sex scenes."

He snorts. "No thanks."

"Snob."

"Have fun. Oh, and Lucy, stop following the cops around town."

I mimic Sally and plug my ears with my fingers. "La-la-la-la ... Can't hear you!" Then I dash out the door to the sound of Will's chuckling.

Chapter Three

I HAVE THIRTY MINUTES to get to book club and I promised Betty Jean I'd bring muffins, so I swing by The Bistro and grab two dozen of my best. Paco watches as I carefully place the muffins in a box. He raises his right paw in the air like he's begging. Either that or he has a question.

I giggle. "What do you want?"

I've only had Paco for a couple of weeks, but in that short time I've learned to read his expressions. This one is what I call his *I want some of that* face.

I have a confession to make. Even though I know I shouldn't, every once in a while, I give Paco an itsy bitsy teeny tiny piece of muffin, but I'm trying to be a good dog mom. Which means no more people food. Even though he seems perfectly fine, my sweet Paco is still recuperating from being poisoned by the same crazy pants who hit me with the frying pan. My vet bill was humungous (not that Paco isn't worth every penny I had to put on my already overloaded credit card).

"You know you're not supposed to eat those. The vet says you need to watch your weight."

Paco sneezes. It sounds like the human equivalent of someone tsking in disgust.

He unleashes the power of those big brown eyes on me. I'm so weak
...

"Okay, okay. Just a little piece. But don't tell Dr. Brooks."

He barks and wags his tail. I break the edge off a banana walnut muffin. He wolfs it down. Then he looks at the box again.

"Oh no. The rest of these are for the book club."

Paco runs to the kitchen door.

"You want to go to book club with me?"

He scratches the door in response.

Why not?

Betty Jean is one of my regular customers, and she seems to really like Paco (one of her few redeeming qualities). "Okay, you can go, but you have to be good. No begging and no interrupting anyone when they're talking. Unless you have something interesting to say about the book."

He barks like he agrees.

I place the muffins in the back of my car, and Paco jumps in the front seat passenger side. It's November, but the weather is Florida cool, not cold tonight, so I roll down the window on his side. Paco is my first dog, but I think sticking your head out the car window is one of those universal dog things.

I've never been to Betty Jean's house, but I know where she lives. Her home is in an older residential neighborhood, just a few blocks from the city park. I come up to a four-way stop sign near the soccer fields when Paco starts barking violently. He lifts himself up by his front paws bringing half his body out the window.

"Paco! What are you doing?"

He turns to look at me and ... oh no. There's a familiar wild glint in his eyes. Before I can stop him, he jumps out the window.

Rats!

I swing my VW beetle to the side of the road, turn off the engine and run after my crazy dog.

"Paco! Come back here this instant!"

It's dark, but the soccer field lights are on so I can see where he's running. He turns his head to check and see if I'm following him, which of course, I am. Then he halts near the edge of a large palm tree.

I stop to catch my breath. "Bad dog! You could have gotten hurt jumping from the car! What were you—"

I stop mid-sentence.

Paco sits there calmly staring down at something.

My skin turns icy cold like I'm in some sort of déjà vu dream. Because that something is a man. And he's not moving.

I kneel down beside him and nudge his shoulder. "Sir, are you all right?"

No response.

I gingerly place my fingers on the side of his neck to check for a pulse, but there isn't one. I roll him over to see if he's breathing and to start CPR.

Holy wow. It's the guy in the blue hoodie.

But no amount of CPR is going to help, because he's got a bullet hole right between his eyes.

Luckily, it takes the cops about three minutes to get here.

Unluckily, it's Travis who responds. I wish it had been Rusty. He's so much easier to manipulate ... I mean, work with.

Travis takes one look at the dead guy and his expression goes grim. "Are you the one who made the call?"

I tell him exactly how things went down, including how Paco led me to the body. This makes two dead bodies that Paco has discovered. I can't snicker anymore at the idea that he might really be a ghost whisperer.

Neither can Travis. "He actually jumped out of the car? And he led you right here. To this exact same spot?" The first time I told Travis that Paco led me to a dead body he practically laughed in my face. Now his disbelief is laced with confusion. Logic tells him that there's no such thing as a ghost whispering dog, but the more intuitive side of him is beginning to wonder.

He glances around the empty soccer field. "Have you seen anyone else?"

"Nope. Just this guy and now you."

He pulls a cell phone from his shirt pocket and spears me with one of his I'm-a-cop-and-you're-a-civilian gazes that he's so good at. "I have to insist that you keep this to yourself."

"This is the guy you and Rusty got the order for this morning."

He stills. "How did you know that?"

Oops. Me and my big mouth. No use in pretending anymore. "Because I followed you."

"You followed me?"

"Not you-you. You and Rusty. That order he put in this morning was ridiculous. Five lattes? C'mon! No self-respecting cop orders a latte when they can get the black swill that passes for coffee down at the station house for free."

"You *followed* a police car?" he asks like he still can't quite believe it.

"Pay attention. Yes, I followed a police car. So what? It's not illegal, is it?"

"It ought to be. You have no idea what you're doing here."

"Okay, so tell me."

"All I can tell you is that you absolutely cannot tell anyone else what you found here tonight."

"Why? Is this guy some kind of police informant? Kitty says he was on his honeymoon, but—"

"Kitty? You called Kitty Pappas?"

"Only because she's the real estate contact for the house."

"My God, you really are dangerous. Haven't we been through this before? Lucy, you need to leave these things—"

"To the professionals? Been there. Done that. Almost got killed."

Travis takes a deep breath like he's trying to keep from saying something he shouldn't. "I admit, I handled Abby Delgado's case poorly. But this is different."

"You didn't handle Abby's case poorly. You just didn't have all the information I did."

He frowns. "What's that supposed to mean?"

Double oops.

The reason I was able to solve Abby's murder was because I used my gift.

"Nothing," I say. "What do you mean this case is different? This is a homicide investigation, right? Who would shoot this poor guy in the head? Do you think he was robbed?"

Whispering Bay is America's safest city? Ha! I wonder how Brittany and the rest of the chamber of commerce are going to spin this. I don't think pruning the trees on Main Street and hanging up a bunch of flowery wreaths are going to cut it.

Before Travis can answer, another police car rolls up. It's Zeke Grant. He's dressed in civilian clothes and the expression on his face is bone weary. Understandable, considering that his wife, Mimi, our city's mayor, gave birth to twins a couple of weeks ago.

"Lucy," he greets me tersely.

"Hi, Zeke." Paco nudges me with his nose as if to remind me that he's still here.

Zeke gazes between Paco and the dead body. "This scenario looks oddly familiar."

I'll say.

"Don't leave just yet," Zeke tells me.

Not a problem, because I have no intention of going anywhere.

Zeke and Travis walk a few feet away and begin to talk. Even though they keep their voices low, I can pick up a few words here and there.

"Anyone called Billings yet?" asks Zeke.

"Right after I called you," says Travis.

I can't make anything else out, but they're acting strange. Very hush-hush. A dark blue sedan pulls up along the street. Two men get out. They're wearing suits and ties. This isn't the same crime scene investigation group I've seen before. For one thing, they aren't wearing uniforms, and they don't seem to have any equipment on them.

The two men glance my way. They walk up to Zeke and Travis. The four of them talk for a few minutes. Then they all turn to look at me. One of the suit guys says something and Travis nods grimly.

Goosebumps erupt over my arms.

Nothing about this scenario makes sense.

Travis breaks away from the group. "Let me take you home."

"No need. I have my car."

"Then let me follow you home and make sure you're okay." He takes me by the elbow and leads me toward my car. It feels more like an order than out of concern for my safety.

We get to the curb and out of earshot from Zeke and the suits before I spin around to face him. "Not so fast, buddy. What's going on? Who are those two guys? Have you called the wife yet to let her know what happened? You need to check out her alibi. They did this entire episode on *America's Most Vicious Criminals* about how most of the time it's the husband or the wife who—"

"Lucy, the guy in the blue hoodie isn't on his honeymoon."

"He's not?"

"His name is Ken Cameron. He was an FBI agent."

Chapter Four

Travis follows me to The Bistro where we go upstairs to my apartment. We settle down on the living room couch with a cup of coffee in our hands.

"Okay, I've been a patient girl, but it's time you told me what's going on."

"The order Rusty and I got this morning was for a group of FBI agents who are here in town."

The hairs on my neck stand on alert. This isn't exactly a lie. But it's not the complete truth either. Travis is hiding something. Too bad for him he doesn't stand a chance against me.

"I see. Like ... an FBI convention?"

"Sure. Yeah. But you know, they don't want to go around announcing they're here, so we need to keep this quiet."

"No problem. You can count on me to keep it on the low down."

He blinks like he's not sure if I'm messing with him or not. "You mean the down-low?"

"Isn't that what I said? So you and Rusty were delivering food to a bunch of agents here on a retreat? That's so sweet of you."

A muscle on the side of his jaw twitches. Travis hates that I've relegated the Whispering Bay police force to a bunch of muffin delivery guys.

"Who do you think killed the guy in the park?" I ask.

"I have no idea. But you can see how important it is to keep this confidential. Since it was an agent, the FBI will be handling this internally."

"Do you think it was a professional hit?"

He looks at me over the rim of his coffee cup. "Possibly."

"I mean, you'd have to be a pretty good shot or just really lucky to get a bullet right between someone's eyes. And the woman who Kitty thinks is the wife? Is she an agent too? How many of them are there?"

"That's a lot of questions, Lucy."

I snort. "You expect me to believe that the FBI is having some kind of agent convention in a house in Dolphin Isles in Whispering Bay, Florida?"

Travis sets his cup down on the coffee table. "Why do you have to make everything so hard?"

"You mean why don't I just believe everything you say?"

"Most women do."

Of all the arrogant ... "Good thing I'm not most women."

We lock gazes. Rats. I'm not purposely flirting. He isn't either. But it just happens.

He closes his eyes for a second like he's recharging. When he opens them again, he's all cop. "Against my better judgment, I'm going to tell you the truth. But only because I know from recent experience that you'll never leave this alone until I do. And you need to leave this alone, or you're going to create a whole lot of trouble for everyone."

I place my coffee mug on the table next to his. "I'm all ears."

He shakes his head like he can't believe what he's about to say. "The FBI is hiding a federal witness here in town."

"Hiding him from what?"

"From certain people who might not want him to testify."

"Certain people? You mean, like … organized crime people?"

He nods.

"So the guy in the park was like … a *mob hit*?"

"Possibly. It's not up to me to say. Or you. Like I said, the FBI will be handling this."

"Who's this guy the FBI is protecting? Some top mob boss who's decided to turn his life around? Is he going into the witness protection program? Is he going to live here in Whispering Bay? Oh my God, what if—"

"It's none of those. And that's all the information you're getting."

"You can't just leave me dangling."

"Sure I can."

I narrow my eyes at him.

"Zeke said I was only to tell you what was absolutely necessary to get your cooperation."

"Well, of course you have my cooperation. But I could do so much more! I could help the FBI—"

"No."

"You didn't let me finish. I could … deliver muffins. Like you did."

"You're not going to deliver muffins to the FBI. Or do anything else for that matter," he adds stubbornly.

I fold my hands demurely on my lap. "Okay. You win. I'll just be a good girl and leave everything to the *professionals*."

Travis moans. I'm sure he's ruing the day he first used that expression on me. "The last time you said that you ended up with a psycho trying to kill you in your own kitchen. Okay. You win. But you have to promise me you'll keep what I tell you confidential. You can't tell anyone. Not your brother. Not Sarah. Not even Will."

I make an X over my chest with my finger. "Cross my heart and hope to die."

"Let's hope it doesn't come down to that," he mutters.

I lean forward eagerly.

"Five years ago, the feds planted a mole by the name of Joey Frizzone in the Scarlotti family organization. They run one of the oldest and largest crime syndicates in Chicago."

"A mole? That's what, like a spy?"

Travis nods. "A few weeks ago, the feds received an anonymous tip that Joey had been compromised, so they had to get him out. He's in hiding until he can testify. The trial is in Chicago in two weeks. After that, they'll put Joey in witness protection. Right now, our goal is to keep him alive so he can put Vito Scarlotti away for good."

"Holy wow."

"That's one way to put it. The Weasel is going to be pretty spooked when he hears what happened to Ken Cameron."

"The weasel?"

"It's the nickname the feds gave Joey."

"Who else knows all this?"

"Here in town? Just Zeke, Rusty and me. And now you."

"No other cops?"

"Billings, she's the FBI agent in charge, only wanted a few cops aware of the situation. In case the feds need police back up."

"What do you think happened to Ken Cameron?"

"I think he got a bullet between the eyes."

"Seriously."

"I think someone has a big mouth," Travis says quietly. The implication being that someone ratted Joey out.

"So someone in the FBI sold The Weasel out to the mob? Do you think they'll move him to another location?"

"Not my call. But moving him might be exactly what someone wants. Until the feds figure out who killed Cameron, they're probably better leaving Joey where he is."

I shudder. "The whole thing sounds dangerous."

"Exactly. Which is why you're going to pretend you don't know anything, didn't see anything, and most importantly, you aren't going to do anything."

"Sure, sure, I got it."

"Repeat it, so I know it's sunk in."

I roll my eyes. "I know nothing. I see nothing. And I'll do nothing."

"You have to act completely normal."

"Normal for me? Or normal for someone else?"

He gives me a look.

"Hey! I'm serious."

"Normal for you. Which is still kind of scary but it's the best we can do." He gets up to leave. Paco and I follow him down the stairs.

Travis reaches the kitchen door, then turns around. "I hate to break our date for Saturday, but with this new development I'm going to be on call twenty-four seven."

"I never said I'd go out with you."

"You would have said yes. Eventually."

"Good to know there's nothing wrong with your ego."

He grins like he thinks I've just made a joke. "Don't forget to lock the door behind me."

"No worries there."

I not only lock it. I check it twice. What a night. This isn't my first dead body, but I'm still pretty shaken up. I hate to admit it, but in this instance, Travis is right. Mobsters in Whispering Bay? I definitely need to leave this to the professionals.

I glance at the kitchen clock. It's nine-thirty. I should probably go to bed since I have an early morning. Or I could blow off some nervous energy perfecting my mango coconut muffin recipe. Or— Oh. My. God.

Book club!

I dash up the stairs with Paco on my heels and dial Betty Jean's number. She picks up on the seventh ring.

"Betty Jean! I'm so sorry I missed the meeting—"

"Lucy, dear, are you in the hospital?"

"Uh, no."

"Is there a psychotic killer holding you hostage in your kitchen again?"

"I can explain."

"I'm listening."

"Well, yeah, there was this emergency you see. The Bistro is all out of flour, and I had to wait here until the delivery truck came by. Can't make muffins without flour." I wince. This is the worst lie ever. And so lame that anyone with half a brain could see right through it. Only I can't very well tell Betty Jean the truth.

"And your cell phone died? And your car ran out of gas? Oh, and let me guess. The dog ate your copy of the book."

"Actually, I have the book on my Kindle, so that would be impossible. I'm so sorry, Betty Jean. I promise this will never happen again."

"Oh, I know it won't, because we won't be inviting you back."

"But—"

"Book club begins promptly at seven p.m. We waited till eight for you and your muffins to show up. I have to tell you, Lucy, we were mightily disappointed. You promised you'd bring some of those new mango coconut muffins you've been bragging about."

"It sounds like it's my muffins you want at book club. Not me."

"Oh, so I'm the bad guy now?"

"No, no, I'm sorry. I didn't mean it the way it sounded. But don't I get a second chance or anything? Please?"

"Sorry, but like I told you, there's a waiting list. You had your chance, Lucy, and you blew it."

Chapter Five

I CAN'T BELIEVE I got kicked out of book club on my first night.

It's embarrassing. Not to mention unfair. If Betty Jean knew the real reason I had to miss last night, she'd be bending over backward kissing my gluteus maximus with her apologies.

The idea that the feds are hiding a Chicago mobster in little old Whispering Bay is unbelievable. It's the second most exciting thing that's ever happened in this town, and I can't tell anyone. Talk about frustrating.

I crawl out of my warm bed, pull on some clothes, then take Paco for his morning walk. It's four-thirty and time to start making the muffins.

Sarah gets to The Bistro around five, and Jill, who works for us, shows up at six to help set up. By seven, we're ready to go and the line to get in this morning is extra-long.

Viola Pantini and her boyfriend Gus Pappas, are the first to arrive. Viola is President of the Gray Flamingos as well as a part-time yoga instructor. I took one of her classes for active and mature adults (she doesn't like to use the word seniors) last week, and I'm embarrassed to say I could hardly keep up. I need to find a class more my speed—like yoga for out-of-shape millennials.

"How are you two doing this morning?" I ask.

Viola smiles cautiously. "We're fine. The question is, how are you, Lucy?"

"Me? I'm great."

Gus and Viola exchange a worried look.

"We heard you got kicked out of Betty Jean's book club," Gus says.

Oh for the love of ...

I grit my teeth. "Who told you that?"

"Victor. We ran into him just now in the parking lot."

Great. Victor Marino is in his sixties. He's a good customer, but he's a member of the Sunshine Ghost Society as well as Betty Jean's book club. If Victor is in the parking lot, that means the rest of his gang isn't far behind. It's like now that they're retired, they've reverted back to high school and can only move in packs of three or more.

He walks through the door, followed by Phoebe Van Cleave. Even though I nabbed a serial killer right beneath her pointy nose, she still hasn't forgiven me for suspecting her of Abby Delgado's murder. It's been a week now. You'd think she'd be over it.

Betty Jean comes next. She walks up to the counter, murmurs her hellos to Viola and Gus then spears me with a look I haven't seen since the kind Mrs. Jackson used to give me back in kindergarten.

"Hello," I say as politely as possible. "What can I get you all this morning?"

Before anyone can put in an order, a big guy with dark hair walks into The Bistro. He's maybe in his late twenties and wearing an Armandi's T-shirt. "Hey! I'm Mike, Rocko's nephew," he booms with a strong New Jersey accent. "Where do you want the goods?"

Yikes. Rocko is our delivery guy. The one who, according to the excuse I gave Betty Jean, already made a delivery last night.

"Oh! Um, you're supposed to park in the back and go in through the kitchen."

"Sorry, but there's a car blocking the way. Not sure I can get the truck in, so I just parked it alongside the road."

Sarah comes flying through the kitchen door. "I saw the delivery truck through the window," she says to me before turning to smile at Mike. "Hello, I'm Sarah. You're filling in for Rocko? He emailed me yesterday and said someone from the family would be taking over his route temporarily?"

"That's me." Mike and Sarah shake hands.

"And you are?" he asks me.

"Lucy McGuffin." Out of the corner of my eye, I can see Betty Jean smirking like she's caught me in a lie. Which, she has.

"I thought you said your delivery person was here last night and that's why you had to miss book club. What was it you said? Can't make the muffins without the flour?"

Everyone turns to look at me, including Mike, who seems confused. Not that I blame him.

Making matters worse, the next customers through the door are none other than my brother Sebastian, and my parents.

"Lucy!" Mom runs behind the counter to give me a big hug.

My parents are what I call reverse snowbirds. After living all their lives in Whispering Bay, George and Molly McGuffin bought a cabin in Maine where they spend summers to avoid the extreme Florida heat and humidity. Now that it's November, they'll be back in town through Memorial Day weekend.

"Are you all right?" Dad asks, following Mom behind the counter. "Sebastian filled us in on what happened last week."

"Lucy, you're a hero!" Mom wipes a tear from the corner of her eye. "I can't believe my baby caught a serial killer! Is your head all right? Sebastian says this woman attacked you with a frying pan! Why didn't you call us? We would have come down immediately."

The hostile looks Betty Jean and Victor were giving me just a minute ago are softened with the reminder that, yeah, I basically saved the town's bacon. Maybe my parents' timing isn't so bad after all.

"I'm fine," I reassure them.

Everyone starts talking at once, welcoming my parents back to town and reliving last week's events. Paco barks to make sure we haven't forgotten about him.

"Is this the dog I've heard so much about?" Mom bends down to scratch Paco behind the ears. He looks up at her with his big brown eyes, and I swear she practically dissolves into a puddle of goo.

"He's adorable! Are you sure you can handle him? On account of your allergies?"

"I'm taking medicine, so yeah, I'm okay."

"Because if you need a home for him, your dad and I could—"

"I'm good, Mom."

Paco, the showboat, wags his tail as if to say mission accomplished! One more fan in town!

The line on the other side of the counter is now longer than ever. "I hate to break this up, but we need to start taking orders again."

Mom pats me on the arm. "We'll catch up later. You and your brother will come to dinner tomorrow." She turns to Sebastian. "Don't forget to invite Will."

Sebastian nods like the good son he is.

"So where do you want me to unload?" Mike asks.

I'd almost forgotten all about him.

Unfortunately, Betty Jean hasn't. "Let me get this straight," she says to Mike. "You made a delivery last night, and now you're making another one? This place sure must use a lot of flour."

I simply cannot help myself. "That's exactly right. He made a delivery last night, and now he's making another one. And *yes*, we do use a lot of flour."

Sarah bites her bottom lip.

I try to whisk Mike away, but Betty Jean is too quick for me. "Is Lucy telling the truth?" she asks him. "Did you make a delivery here last night?" Her eyes glitter in evil anticipation. It's not enough that she's kicked me out of her book club. Now she plans to humiliate me in front of half the town, my parents included, by exposing my big fat lie.

I cringe, waiting for the ax to fall.

"Yeah, that's right," Mike says. "I was here last night. But the order was wrong, so I had to bring the rest of it this morning."

What?

Did Rocko's nephew just lie for me?

I had no idea I was holding my breath until now.

"Sorry again for the inconvenience," Mike improvises. "Rocko would kill me if he knew I'd messed up. If you want to show me where to bring in the stuff, I can get out of your hair."

Betty Jean's mouth sets into a grim line. I'm still not out of the hot seat because in her mind I should have called to excuse myself, but at least she can't accuse me of lying to her.

I walk Mike through the kitchen and out to the back parking lot. He's right. There are too many cars to allow him to get his truck in here. "I got a dolly I can put the supplies on," he says. "No big deal to unload the truck where it is and haul the stuff in that way."

"Thanks. And, *um*, thank you for backing me up out there."

He shrugs. "Hey, we all have our secrets."

"It's … complicated, but suffice it to say I was supposed to be somewhere last night and used your delivery service as an excuse."

"So I was probably the last person you wanted to see this morning, huh?"

"Not necessarily. We're running low on chocolate chips."

He chuckles. "You're funny, Lucy." He looks at me longer than necessary making my cheeks go warm. He's a big guy. Not fat, but solid. His nose is crooked like it's been broken and didn't heal properly.

"Where's Rocko?" I ask. "He's okay, isn't he?"

"Yeah, sure. He's on a long overdue vacation."

The hairs on my neck tingle. This is a lie, but it's not a big one. Maybe it's private family business, so I shrug it off.

He goes out to the truck and comes back with a loaded dolly. "Where do you want all this?"

I show him the pantry. Mike puts away all the supplies, cuts down the boxes, and even offers to haul a load of trash out to the dumpster, which isn't in his job description, but he insists. After he takes out our trash, he lingers for a few minutes like he doesn't want to leave just yet, so I offer him a cup of coffee.

"What was all that about you being a hero?" he asks.

I flush. "Oh, that." I give him the short version of how I solved Abby's murder and nabbed a serial killer at the same time.

Mike looks impressed. "Remind me not to mess with you, Lucy."

"Oh, you're safe from me. Unless you're planning on killing someone?" I tease.

"Not today," he says with a straight face.

I laugh at his joke and then because I catch him ogling a batch of pumpkin spice muffins cooling on a rack, reach over and hand him one.

He takes a bite of the muffin and makes what I like to call the yummy face, except on Mike it looks funny on account of his crooked nose. Still, I can't help but feel pleased.

"You made this?"

"I make all the muffins and the baked goods and some of the sandwiches. Sarah makes all the rest. If you're a mac and cheese kind of person, you won't find any better than hers."

He glances around the kitchen. The dining area in The Bistro has a beach theme—brightly colored walls with murals of dolphins, but the kitchen is all business. High-end stainless-steel appliances and three industrial ovens. "Where did you learn to cook like this?"

"Culinary school, but I've been hooked on baking since my first job washing dishes at The Harbor House."

"That's my next drop off."

"I bet they get some big orders, huh?"

"Yeah, I guess. So you like working here?"

"I love being my own boss. And I love baking. And I really like interacting with customers. The only downfall is the four-thirty a.m. wake up call. Otherwise, it's pretty much perfect."

He grins. "Yeah, Rocko's route starts at five, so I can sympathize."

"My only day off is Sunday, and even then, I'm up by five. Habit, I guess."

We chat a bit more, mostly about me and my kitchen, which is flattering. He tells me he's from New Jersey and that he's temporarily staying with his parents a half hour away in Panama City. Before he leaves, I check to make sure we got everything on the list and sign the order form.

"See you in a few days," he says.

"Hold on." I grab a few of my best muffins and place them in a bag. "In case you get hungry later. My way of saying thanks, for, you know, backing up my story."

"Thanks, Lucy." Then he winks at me and heads out the door.

That night I have trouble sleeping which is unusual for me. Between my early morning hours and the medication I have to take because of the dog allergies, I usually hit my pillow in a semi-comatose state.

Was Rocko's nephew flirting with me? I mean, a wink doesn't necessarily mean anything, but I'm still not sure why he backed up my lie.

Oh well. Maybe I should just chalk it up to good luck. Which I'm definitely due for considering that in the past two weeks I've come across two dead bodies. Or rather, Paco has. All of which means I can no longer ignore the fact that my dog has some serious skills. Skills that, combined with mine, could come in handy when investigating a murder.

Not that I'm going to investigate anything. Nope. I promised Travis I'd keep my nose out of this and I meant it. I do *not* need to get involved here.

Still. Poor Ken Cameron. One minute you're babysitting a mobster and eating muffins, and the next you've got a bullet between the eyes. The whole thing seems unfair.

Chapter Six

THE NEXT MORNING EVERYTHING goes back to normal. Or as normal as it can be considering that the feds are hiding a mobster in the middle of a suburban neighborhood and that an FBI agent has been assassinated in the city's park. But since no one knows this except a handful of people, the town is oblivious. My fifteen minutes of fame are clearly over because the early breakfast crowd is back to just regular busy.

I'm in between orders, manning the counter, still trying to figure out if Mike Armandi was flirting with me when the door to The Bistro opens and in come two unfamiliar faces. One is smiling at me like she knows me and we're best friends. The other one looks like he just ate a worm, and not the kind that comes in a tequila bottle.

"Lucy! It's really you! You look just like in your audition tape!" says the woman. Mid-thirties, short platinum blonde hair, super thin, wire-rim glasses.

Even though I've never met her before, I recognize her, as well. The voice is too distinctive for this to be anyone but Tara Bell, a producer for the Cooking Channel.

"Tara?"

"In the flesh, baby!"

Her companion is loaded down with some fancy looking camera equipment. Late twenties, tall, man bun.

Does Brittany know they're here?

I gulp. "We weren't expecting you until Monday."

"I know! Ha-ha! But what's the point of doing a film test when you know we're coming? We want to capture The Bistro's natural vibe. The everyday mojo between you and your customers. Not some contrived environment. Can you believe one town we almost picked had all the businesses put big red bows on their front doors before we came to film? Ha-ha! As if I couldn't see right through that phony baloney."

Yikes. "Who would do that? Not anyone in Whispering Bay."

"Exactly! I've been in this town all of thirty minutes, and I can already tell this place is real. As in R-E-A-L," she says spelling out the word.

Paco runs up to her and starts barking. Not angry barking, but he's not wagging his tail either.

"Who's this little fella? Aren't you just a-dor-a-ble? You're like a teeny tiny little ba-by wa-by!"

Hmmm .... Tara sure does seem to have a lot of energy.

Paco stops barking and stares like he doesn't know what to make of this baby talk.

"This is my dog, Paco. He lives with me in the apartment upstairs. The customers seem to like him."

"A dog, here in the café? So like every day is Bring Your Dog to Work Day! I love it! It's so *now*! So hip! Wade!" she snaps at Man Bun. "Make sure you get the dog in lots of footage!"

Ha! Too bad Brittany isn't here for this.

"So, my guy here—what's your name again? Why is my film crew always quitting on me? Oh yeah, it's Wade, right? Say hi, Wade!" she orders.

Man Bun mumbles something under his breath that sounds like "The name is Wayne." He barely glances at me. "Hey."

"So, as I was saying, Wade is going to set up the equipment and you and your customers just ignore us. Yep, just go about your business making lattes or whatever else it is you do, and we'll just do our thing too."

Sarah pokes her head out the kitchen door.

"You must be the other one!" Tara grabs Sarah's hand and pumps it up and down vigorously. "Tara Bell, Cooking Channel producer. Got your signature on all our papers, so we're good to go."

"Hello," Sarah says, looking confused.

I explain what's going on.

"We thought you'd be here Monday."

"They all do!" Tara starts laughing like a hyena. I don't know what she's smoking, but I'm pretty sure it isn't legal yet in Florida.

I try to do what Tara asks by ignoring her and the guy with the camera.

Our customers, however, are a different story.

Viola comes up to the counter to ask for extra cream. "Lucy, dear, who is that strange woman standing in the corner looking at everyone and taking notes? She seems a bit intense."

"She's a producer from the Cooking Channel. She and her crew are here to take some spontaneous footage. It's part of the audition process for *Battle of the Beach Eats*."

"You mean, we're on camera?"

I nod.

"I wish I'd known! I would have had my hair done."

"I think they're looking for spontaneity."

The door to The Bistro opens and Brittany dashes in. She's wearing a black pencil skirt and four-inch heels. It also looks like she went to the salon and got a blowout. Her auburn hair is sleek and shiny, whereas my brown curly hair is stuffed beneath a sweaty baseball cap. If this weren't her everyday look, I'd think that Brittany knew something I didn't.

She takes one look at Tara and freezes. "Oh my God. It's true. They're here." Brittany smooths down her skirt and smiles for the camera, something she's had a lot of practice with since she's a former Miss Cheese Grits. She's won other pageants as well, but that title is my personal favorite.

Tara waves to us from across the room. "Hey, girls! Keep doing what you're doing, and we'll keep doing our thing too!"

"What's going on?" Brittany asks without moving her lips and smiling at the same time. It's an impressive skill. This must have been her pageant talent.

I try to do the magic lip thing too, but after flubbing the first couple of words, I give up. "Tara and her film crew are here early."

"Well, *obviously*. But why?"

"Because they want us to be real and spontaneous."

Brittany keeps smiling in case the camera catches her. "I need to go warn the other restaurants in town. Make sure to keep her here as long as possible."

"How am I supposed to do that? I've got a business to run."

"I don't know!" she whispers-shouts still doing her ventriloquist act. "Just. Do. It."

I feel like I should salute, but I restrain myself. "I'll try my best."

She waves goodbye to Tara. "Nice seeing you!"

"Ciao!" Tara bellows as Brittany makes her escape.

I don't think keeping Tara and Man Bun here will be a problem since they've pretty much made themselves at home. Man Bun puts his camera down for a minute to order a coffee and a breakfast sandwich. I hope this isn't some kind of secret taste test. Not that Sarah's breakfast sandwiches aren't to die for, but I wish we'd been given a bit more warning. It's not fair that Tara came to our place first and that Brittany is giving the other restaurants in the competition a heads up.

"Want a muffin with your sandwich?" I ask Man Bun.

"What kind you got?"

I point to the handwritten menu on the chalkboard above his head. "Today's special is the pumpkin spice, but we also have blueberry, double chocolate chip, and apple walnut cream cheese." The only reason I put blueberry muffins on the menu is because so many people like them, but personally, I find them boring.

"I'll try the blueberry," he says.

Figures.

"Wade!" Tara screeches from across the café startling everyone within a half mile. "Keep filming!"

Three people from the back of the café get up to leave. On their way out the door they shake their heads at me as if this invasion of their privacy is somehow my fault.

Thanks a lot, Cooking Channel.

I give Man Bun his order, and he manages to both eat and film at the same time.

Then Rusty and Travis walk in. It's the first time I've seen Travis since the night I discovered Ken Cameron's body. Paco runs over to greet them.

Travis scratches Paco in his favorite spot behind his ears. 'Hey, Lucy."

"Hi," I say trying to act "normal" per his previous instructions. "What'll it be today?"

Rusty pulls a paper from his pocket. "Six lattes, two dozen muffins—assorted but heavy on the double chocolate chip--four turkey sandwiches, and three tubs of Sarah's mac and cheese."

Six lattes? It's hard not to smirk at this ridiculousness. "And this will be to go?" I ask punching the order into the computer.

"Yep," says Travis. As if he senses someone behind him, he turns to find Man Bun pointing a camera at him.

"Get that thing out of my face," Travis warns.

"Chill out. Just act natural, dude."

"What's going on?" asks Rusty.

"This is the crew from the Cooking Channel. They're here today to take some footage of the café."

Tara saunters over to the counter. "We'll be filming all the participating restaurants in town," she explains. "It will help us decide whether or not we want to pick Whispering Bay for our next season of *Battle of the Beach Eats*."

Rusty puffs out his chest. "Russell Newton, twenty-two-year veteran of the Whispering Bay Police Department at your service," he says directly into the camera.

"Nice to meet you, Russell!" Tara says. "But we don't want you talking to the camera. You're supposed to pretend like we're not here."

"Oh. Sorry." Rusty looks off in the other direction, but it looks awkward like he's avoiding the camera which is the exact opposite of what Tara is going for.

Travis looks tense. Not that I blame him. Here they are on a super top-secret mission to get muffins for Joey "The Weasel" and his FBI team, and they're being filmed while doing it.

"Who's going to be looking at this film?" he asks.

"Just me and a few other producers from the network," says Tara. She studies Travis with interest. "Has anyone ever told you that you look like Ryan Reynolds?"

"Doesn't he?" says Betty Jean, who I hadn't noticed before in line. "I was the first one in town to point it out."

Tara hands Travis a business card. "I also do some freelance work for the Bravo channel. They're looking for eligible guys for a new reality dating show. Interested? If you're single, I can practically guarantee you a spot."

"I'd be interested," says Rusty. "Only don't tell my girlfriend. She'd skin me alive."

Tara ignores Rusty. "So, what do you say?" she asks Travis.

"Thanks, but the answer is no."

Sarah comes out from the kitchen with two big paper bags and hands them to Travis, who thanks her. "Let's go," he says to Rusty. "See you later, Lucy."

I wave goodbye as they head out. Too bad I didn't have a chance to ask Travis how things were progressing in the Ken Cameron investigation. Although I doubt he'd tell me anything anyway.

Sally from the library comes up to the counter to order. "Hey, Lucy! I'll have a double chocolate chip muffin and a coffee. To go." She glances back at the door. "Who were those cops I just saw on my way in? One of them is really cute."

"The older one is Rusty Newton, and the younger one is Travis Fontaine. He's new in town too."

"Married?"

"I assume you're asking about Travis and not Rusty?" I tease.

She makes a face. "Yeah."

"Not married."

"Girlfriend?"

It occurs to me that this might be the perfect solution to my Travis problem. Sally is probably around thirty. She's cute and smart and funny. She and Travis would be perfect together. "He's single and completely available."

"*Nice.* I was beginning to think this town might be too dull for me. Now I just have to figure out how to run into that hunka-hunka burning love again and make him fall at my feet."

I laugh because it seems like the polite thing to do, but it's not *that* funny. I mean, sure. Travis is great looking but he also has a brain.

I hand Sally her coffee and muffin. "Thanks." She lowers her voice. "Betty Jean was at the library yesterday afternoon. She told everyone who'd listen that she kicked you out of her book club. What happened?"

Since I can't tell Sally about finding Ken Cameron dead in the park, I have to keep up the lie I've told everyone else. "I got distracted by a late delivery here at The Bistro and forgot all about the book club meeting. By the time I called to apologize she was pretty upset."

"And the old bat kicked you out because of that?"

"Apparently there's a long waiting list to join."

Sally shakes her head in disgust. "Geez."

An idea occurs to me. "Hey, maybe we can start our own book club. I have a few friends who might be interested."

"Yeah, that sounds great!"

The little hairs on my neck tingle. Sally isn't interested in starting a book club with me. This is one of those times that I hate my gift. Here we were having a perfectly lovely conversation, and I catch her in a lie.

My ego might be bruised because I thought she liked me, but my brain tells me that I shouldn't take it personally. Sally works all day in a library. The last thing she probably wants is to spend an evening with a bunch of women discussing books. I would react the same way if someone asked me to join a baking club.

Despite Tara and Man Bun's in-your-face presence, the rest of the morning goes by uneventfully. I'm about to take a break when Jim Fontaine comes in.

"How's the head, Lucy?" Jim is Travis's dad. Even though I've only known him a couple of weeks, he's already one of my favorite people.

"Better today, thanks."

"Glad to hear that." He orders coffee and a muffin.

"What kind would you like?"

"Surprise me," he says, his green eyes friendly. It's amazing how much father and son look alike, except Jim's eyes give off a warm and cozy vibe, whereas Travis's gaze is fierce. Except when it's warm. Like the night I thought he was going to kiss me.

Nope. I'm not going to think about that right now.

I hand over an apple walnut cream cheese muffin because you can't go wrong with that.

"Have you taken a break this morning? I'd love to have you join me."

"Perfect timing," I say, handing off counter duty to Sarah.

Jim and I get a table in the back. We try to avoid Tara, but it's impossible.

"Have you seen Wade?" she asks. "I tell you, the help you get these days. No one takes their job seriously. If he doesn't watch it, he's going straight back to the public access channel."

"The last time I saw him he was in the pantry. I think."

"Where's that?" she demands.

So far, Tara and Man Bun have been all over the dining area, the kitchen, our bathrooms. The only place they haven't been is upstairs in my apartment (that I know of). What more are they looking for?

And better yet, why don't they leave already? How much footage do these people need?

I sigh. "The pantry? It's just off the kitchen. Ask Sarah. She'll show you. Now if you don't mind, I'm taking a break."

"What's that all about?" Jim asks as soon as Tara is out of earshot.

I explain all about the audition for the Cooking Channel show.

Jim settles into his chair. "I heard from a buddy of mine back in Dallas who worked the Angel of Death case with me. He's pretty impressed with how you were able to figure it out."

"I got lucky is all."

He takes a sip of his coffee then places his cup down to give me a thoughtful look. "Your special skill definitely helped." When I first told Jim about my gift, he was skeptical. Not that I blame him. But he quickly came around after I solved the decades-old case. "Does Travis know? About how you're able to—"

"God no!"

Jim raises a brow at what must seem like an overreaction on my part.

"It's just that ... he'd probably find it hard to believe."

"I get it. But you should consider telling him, Lucy. He's beating himself up thinking that he missed some big clue while investigating Abby's murder. He feels responsible for the danger you were in."

"He shouldn't."

"I agree." Jim smiles kindly. "Regardless, it's your secret to share. Not mine." He fiddles with his coffee mug for a few seconds before he says, "Travis told me that the two of you are going out."

"Oh, he did, did he?"

Jim stills. "Uh-oh, looks like I spoke out of turn."

"Your son asked. I said no. I'm flattered, but I'm *um*, just not interested." The minute I say it, I realize how insulting that might sound. Travis is Jim's only son. He probably thinks he walks on water.

"Not that Travis isn't a great guy," I say. "Any girl would be lucky to go out with him. It's just that ... I'm already seeing someone."

Yikes. I hate lying to Jim, but this is one of those times that telling a little white fib will make someone feel better, so it's for a good cause.

Jim's eyes fill with understanding. "Will Cunningham," he says. "I suspected that you might have feelings for him, but Travis insisted that you were only friends."

"You and Travis have talked about Will and me?" I croak.

"Only because he asked me for advice."

My stomach suddenly feels the way it does when I've eaten too much raw muffin batter (I know, I know, I'm not supposed to do that).

Jim thinks I have feelings for Will. Am I that obvious?

And why is Travis so sure that Will and I are only friends? Unless he and Will have talked about me too. They're in the same basketball league, so they've definitely spent time together. Will must have told Travis that his feelings for me are strictly platonic. It's the reason Travis is so confident that I'll go out with him.

"I'm not dating Will," I say as firmly as possible. "It's someone else, but, it's in the early stages so I'd rather not discuss it."

Jim politely changes the subject just like I knew he would.

We spend a few more minutes chatting about nothing in particular. A part of me wishes I could sink into the floor for lying to Jim about this new mysterious boyfriend of mine, and another part wishes I could get his thoughts about the dead FBI agent, but I promised Travis I wouldn't tell anyone and that includes his father.

Jim finishes his late morning breakfast. When I get back to the counter, Brittany is waiting for me. "Lucy!" she hisses. "What's Tara still doing here?"

"What happened to keep them here as long as possible?"

"I didn't mean for you to monopolize them! Never mind, at least I was able to warn all the other restaurants in town. I just wish we'd gotten those wreaths in time. They're completely adorable."

"I don't think wreaths on the door are going to matter to Tara and the people at the Cooking Channel. They're looking for—"

"Of course it matters! Looks are *everything*!"

"Are you going to order something or not? Because I'm busy."

Brittany looks hurt by my snappiness.

"Sorry," I mutter, "You're right, the wreaths would have been a game changer."

She accepts my apology with a sniff. "I guess while I'm here I might as well eat something. Can I have the turkey Rueben sandwich, only without the bread and the cheese and the sauerkraut?"

"That just leaves the turkey."

"Perfect!"

No wonder Brittany is a size two. I make her a turkey lettuce wrap, and she takes a seat in the middle of the café. Probably so she can keep an eye on Tara.

Sarah and I switch up spots, with me in the kitchen and her manning the counter. I prep up some sandwiches and clean up the area by the fridge. Our trash is overflowing, so I bag it up and head outside to the back parking lot with Paco alongside me.

It's the first time I've been out in the sun today. I turn my face toward the sky and shut my eyes to bask in the gorgeous November weather and catch up on my Vitamin D.

Paco starts barking violently.

My eyes fly open.

What's going on?

He's sitting in front of the dumpster, and he's acting strangely, as if

...

My skin goes clammy.

"What's wrong, boy?" I walk toward him and set the trash bag on the ground. Now that I'm standing next to the dumpster, Paco goes quiet. He sits there patiently, waiting.

I take a deep breath.

Even though a part of me says this really can't be happening, another part (the part that listens to my Spidey sense) warns me exactly what I'm about to find. Like I said, my dog has *skills*.

I say a quick Hail Mary in my head, then open the lid to the dumpster.

A man stares back at me. Only there's a bullet hole between his eyes so I don't think he can actually see me.

I gulp. This makes the third dead body that Paco has led me to. The Sunshine Ghost Society is right. Paco is a ghost whisperer.

Holy wow. My dog is like supernatural or something.

I don't know why I've fought this. If I can be a human lie detector, then Paco can certainly be on speaking terms with Casper.

"What are you doing?"

I jump at the sound of Tara's voice. Man Bun aims his camera at the dumpster.

"I think you better turn off the camera."

Tara's eyes go wide. "Why? What's going on?"

"Let's just say things here at The Bistro have gotten a little *too* real."

Chapter Seven

WITHIN FIVE MINUTES OF calling Travis, he and Zeke show up. I tell them exactly what happened, down to the last detail.

"The dog led you to the dead body?" Zeke says. "Again?"

"Yep. Well, I was going to empty the trash anyway, so I would have found it eventually, but yes, Paco already knew it was there."

"Because of this signal you say he gives you?"

"Like I said before, he begins to bark in this weird way then he shows me where he wants me to go and when I get there, he stops barking and waits."

Zeke shakes his head like he's not sure who's wackier, me for believing this, or him for listening to it.

Travis looks between me and Paco, then me again. This time there's no disbelief in his gaze. Just stunned confusion. I think he finally gets it, only his brain is having a hard time accepting it.

Zeke makes a call on his cell. Within fifteen minutes an army of suits swarms down on the café including the two from the park the other night. They identify themselves as part of an elite state-run CSI team, only I know better. Clearly, they don't want anyone knowing they're with the FBI. Which must mean the guy in the dumpster has something to do with Joey. They ask everyone in the café to stay inside. Although *ask* is the wrong word here. It's more like an order.

"I demand to speak to a lawyer!" shrieks Tara. The second the suits showed up, they confiscated all the film Man Bun worked so hard getting today. She paces up and down the café, and everyone, including Betty Jean, is a little afraid of her right now. "Does the ACLU know what's going on? Freedom of the press, baby! Ever heard of it?"

"Drug test," Travis snaps back. "Ever heard of that?"

Tara goes pale. She meekly sits down but not before muttering, "You can forget being cast on that new Bravo show." Brittany immediately runs over to commiserate, or rather, suck up to her.

The two suits from the park usher me into the kitchen. Now that we're alone and out of view from the customers, one of them flashes an FBI badge in my face. "I'm Agent Parks, and this is Agent Rollins. First off, you absolutely cannot reveal that we're with the Bureau. We're on an undercover mission here." They remind me of those clones from The Matrix except they're not wearing sunglasses.

"I haven't told anyone about Ken Cameron, have I?"

Agent Parks narrows his eyes at me. "This is the second dead body in two days. You don't find it strange that you're the one who's discovered them both?"

"No. And it's my dog who found them. Is that another FBI agent out there in the dumpster?"

"We can't answer that question," says Agent Rollins.

The little hairs on my neck tell me what he won't. The guy in the dumpster isn't with the FBI. But if he isn't an agent, then why is the FBI here? Who is he? Nobody I've ever seen around town. A tourist, maybe?

This is definitely not good for business.

"When was the last time you took out the garbage?" asks Agent Parks.

"You mean before just now? That would be yesterday afternoon."

"Have you seen anyone acting suspiciously?"

"Not really. Do you think that poor man was killed here, in the parking lot?"

"We can't—"

"Answer that. Don't you think this is a bit one sided? I'm supposed to give you all this information, but you guys give me squat in return?"

They ignore my concern, ask me a few more questions, then go off to interview the rest of the café. Brittany takes this opportunity to find me in the kitchen. "This is awful! How could you let this happen?"

"Let what—you mean the dead guy? It's not like I planned this."

"Tara says she doesn't want anything to do with us!" Tears fill Brittany's eyes. "She's going to recommend to the other producers that they pick Catfish Cove instead of us."

"Guess I can't blame her."

"Can't blame her! You sound like you don't even care. This stint on the Cooking Channel was going to prove to everyone that ... You do know what everyone in town is saying behind my back, don't you?"

"What do you mean?"

"They're saying the only reason I got the job with the Chamber of Commerce is because of Daddy's influence."

"Well—"

"I've busted my derriere for this city!" The tears flow faster now.

I hand Brittany a Kleenex. "Well of course I care. I want to win *Battle of the Beach Eats* just as much as anyone else." Not to mention the twenty-five grand which I was practically counting on.

Brittany wipes her eyes. "Then we need to do something quick."

"Like what? It's not like I can undo finding a dead guy during my mid-morning break."

Her face sets with determination. "We need to convince Tara that Whispering Bay is still her best option, which means we need to dig up some dirt on Catfish Cove. I checked out their chamber of commerce website the other day. Can you believe their city's tagline is The Fishing Capital of the Southeast? Ha! Sorry, but America's Safest City is so much better."

After the events of the past few weeks, I'm not sure our city's tagline is so accurate anymore, but the last thing I want to do right now is mention this to Brittany.

"Dig up dirt on Catfish Cove? So, all we have to do is find something worse than a dead body in the dumpster?"

"Now you're getting the hang of it."

"I was being sarcastic. I don't think you can get worse than a murder in town."

"Oh, it could be worse. We just have to find out what that is. We can do this!" Brittany says with all the enthusiasm of her former head cheerleading days. "We can still save our slot on *Battle of the Beach Eats*."

"You think so?"

"I know so!" She reaches out and grabs me in a tight hug. "There's no one else I'd rather go through a crisis with than you, Lucy. I'm so glad we're best friends now!"

After what seems like forever, the suits let the customers go home. They finish taking pictures and collecting evidence and leave an unwanted "gift" in the form of yellow crime tape wrapped around the building and the parking lot. We might as well put up a big sign that says Stay Away—Something Bad Happened Here!

Sarah and I are told that the café has to remain closed until further notice, but "hopefully" we can reopen sometime next week. Most people would relish the time off, but between the loss of business and the bad press we're surely going to get (because, *hello*, dead body in the dumpster) things aren't looking too peachy right now.

Add in the fact that I can no longer count on the chance I might have had for the twenty-five grand if we'd won *Battle of the Beach Eats*. Sure, Brittany thinks she can change Tara's mind and still get us on the show, but c'mon, I have a more realistic view of life.

The Bistro on the Beach is doomed.

Or rather, my personal finances are. When Sarah and I bought this place six months ago, it was Whispering Bay's most popular casual eatery. It still is, at least, I hope so, but the mortgage is humongous. I sunk everything I had into my share of the down payment and still had to borrow money from Will. Add in my credit card debt, and I pretty much live paycheck to paycheck.

Sarah and I are alone in the kitchen tidying up.

"Are you okay?" she asks cutting through the gloomy silence.

"Why wouldn't I be?"

She folds her arms across her chest. Sarah is only a few years older than me and her beautiful blonde self hardly looks the motherly type, but she's one of the kindest people I know. "You just found a dead body less than a week after being attacked in this very kitchen. You have to be freaked out here."

Two dead bodies, I want to say, but I'm not supposed to tell anyone about Ken Cameron.

"I'm a little freaked out," I admit. "But I'm all right."

"Everything is cleaned up and ready to go for Monday, but I guess we won't be open, so..."

"What are we going to do?"

She pats me on the shoulder. "We'll be fine, Lucy."

Sarah will be fine. Her husband is rich. But me? I'm not so sure.

"I was going to head out, but I hate to leave you here alone," she says.

Paco barks as if to say he's got it covered.

Sarah laughs. "Okay, you're not exactly alone." She picks up her bag and fishes out her car keys. "If you need anything or want to sleep somewhere else, you can always crash at my place. Luke's away for a couple of days on a business trip so we could have some girl time. We could watch Hallmark movies and drink wine and eat chocolate for dinner."

I smile. "It sounds fabulous and I'm definitely tempted, but I'm going to my parents for dinner tonight."

She hugs me and makes me promise to call her if I need anything.

I'm about to head up the stairs to my apartment to shower when there's a hard knock on the kitchen door. I freeze. Okay, maybe Sarah's right. Maybe I am just a little more than freaked out here, but who wouldn't be?

"Lucy, it's me," Travis says through the door.

Whew.

I open the door to find Travis and a woman I've never seen before.

Chapter Eight

THE WOMAN IS DRESSED in black pants and a blazer. Late thirties, light brown hair pulled back in a tight bun, clear gray eyes that mean serious business. She shows me her FBI badge. "Agent Patricia Billings. You can call me Billings."

"Nice to meet you. I'm Lucy—"

"McGuffin," she finishes as she walks into my kitchen. "I need to talk to you. Fontaine here says you might be able to assist us."

It's about time someone in law enforcement shows some appreciation for my skills. "Anything to help the FBI," I say. "What do you need me to do?"

"You've found two dead bodies of great interest to the Bureau. Is that a coincidence?"

"What's that supposed to mean?"

Paco scrunches his nose at her.

Agent Billings notices him for the first time. "Cute dog," she says dismissively. "It means that somehow you've managed to be in the right place at the right time."

"Or the wrong place at the wrong time. Believe me, I don't get my jollies discovering dead bodies."

She cocks her head toward Travis. "Fontaine says that you solved a murder here last week. I've looked you up, McGuffin. You caught the Angel of Death serial killer, something the FBI has been trying to do for over a decade. How did you do it?"

I thought when she asked for my help, she meant doing something fun, liking assisting in a stake out. But all she wants to do is interrogate me.

"I got lucky."

"Lucky? I don't think so." She walks through the kitchen and out into the dining area like she owns the place. Travis and I automatically follow. She glances up the stairs. "You live here too?"

I reluctantly nod. This woman is giving off an unfriendly vibe. Paco feels it too. He's not barking, but he hasn't taken his eyes off her since she's walked through the door like he's suspicious of her every move. Right now, he's the canine equivalent of Robert DeNiro from *Meet The Parents*. If he could do the two fingers V sign for *I'm watching you*, he would.

"Mind if I check out your place?" Without waiting for an answer, she starts climbing the stairs to my apartment.

I dash ahead and block her from my door. "Yes, I mind. What are you looking for exactly?"

For a second she looks startled, like she's not used to anyone telling her no, but she regroups fast enough. "What are you? Some sort of hacker? How were you able to solve a case that highly trained professional FBI agents weren't able to crack?"

"Hacker?" I snort. "Lady, I can barely keep my online checking account straight."

"Lucy hasn't done anything illegal," Travis says in my defense. "She's really smart. And able to read people better than anyone I've ever met."

Aw. Hearing Travis stick up for me makes my insides go warm and fuzzy. But I'm still not going out with him.

Agent Billings looks me over like I'm a bug under her microscope. "Are you going to help us or not?" she demands.

"I've already answered all your questions. Other than that, I'm not sure what I can do." I open the door to my apartment and usher them inside. Normally, when I invite someone to my place, I offer them something to drink, but I'm exhausted, and Agent Billings can get her own friggin' coffee. Preferably somewhere else.

She sits on my couch. "It goes against every instinct to bring a civilian in on this, but I have no choice. Fontaine told me that you've already been filled in on the Joey Frizzone situation. The man you found in the park? Ken Cameron? He was my partner." Her voice hitches for a second. Blue Hoodie guy was her partner? Man, that must be tough. I cut her some slack.

"I don't intend to lose any more agents," she says. "Or Joey, either. It's imperative we keep The Weasel safe. His testimony will be the result of over five years of work for the Bureau."

"Sure, I understand. So, what does all this mean? Who's the guy in the dumpster?"

"The man you found today was no FBI agent. His name is Mark Rinaldi. He's a professional hitman. Or rather, he was."

"Do you think he's the one who killed Ken Cameron?"

She hesitates. "No."

"But you do think this Mark Rinaldi was here to kill Joey?"

"Definitely."

"But ... that makes no sense. I mean, I get why this Rinaldi character wants to kill Joey. Money, right?"

"Word on the street is that Vito Scarlotti has put a half-million-dollar contract on Joey's life. No questions asked."

"Holy wow. For half a mil I'll kill him myself."

Agent Billings raises a brow at me.

I clear my throat. "Just kidding." Sort of.

"So what was the motive to kill Mark Rinaldi? And Ken Cameron?"

"Very few people know where Joey is, but obviously the word leaked out."

"You think Agent Cameron ratted Joey out? For money?"

Her gray eyes blaze with fury. "Absolutely not. Ken was an upstanding guy. The best. But … he could be sloppy sometimes."

Oh. I get it now. "The two of you were more than partners?"

"We were friends," she says simply.

A lot more than friends if my Spidey sense is on track here. My sympathy for her goes up a couple more notches.

"Ken—I mean, Agent Cameron must have let Joey's location slip," she says. "He probably realized it, but before he could warn any of us, he was killed to keep him quiet."

An interesting theory. But I have another one too. One that isn't so nice. One that involves Ken Cameron selling Joey out for money and then being double-crossed.

"But what was the motive to kill Mark Rinaldi?" I ask, confused.

"Rinaldi was killed by another hitman."

"Another hitman?" I squeak. This is getting worse by the second.

"Every thug with a five-cent brain is probably on their way here now to Whispering Bay to take out The Weasel. Five hundred thousand dollars is a huge incentive." She glances at Travis, then her gaze goes back to me. "Both Agent Cameron and Mark Rinaldi were killed by the same person. A bullet hole clean between the eyes is the trademark work of a deadly assassin who goes by the name El Tigre. He's based out of New York and works primarily for the Russian mob, but Vito's half-million must have been too big a temptation."

"The Tiger, huh? What does he look like?" Because this is someone I probably want to avoid.

"No one has ever seen El Tigre. At least, no one who's lived to tell about it."

"So this El Tigre killed Mark Rinaldi as a warning?"

"El Tigre killed Rinaldi to get him out of the way. The warning, as you put it, was dumping the body in a public place. He wants to make sure everyone in town knows he's here. It's his way of telling any other contenders that Joey is his hit, and anyone who gets in his way is going to end up in a dumpster like Rinaldi."

I shudder. *Correction*: El Tigre is definitely someone I want to avoid.

"If you don't know what he looks like, how can you catch him?"

Agent Billings narrows her eyes at me. "Because you've seen him."

"*Me*? What are you talking about?"

"Part of El Tigre's M.O. is that he always dumps a body in a place he knows. Leaving Mark Rinaldi in your dumpster wasn't a coincidence. El Tigre was here to scope the place out beforehand. Most likely as a customer."

"You mean I served him coffee?" I shudder. "I wish I could help you, but I can't think of anyone who's come in here who looks like a psychopathic killer."

"But then, you didn't suspect the Angel of Death until you caught her, did you?"

She makes a good point.

"El Tigre is smart. He could be disguised as almost anyone. Some meek mannered tourist, perhaps."

"It sounds like it's going to be almost impossible to fish this guy out. Why not just whisk Joey to another location? Wouldn't that solve your problem?"

"The judge has moved up the trial date, so we only need to keep Joey here a few more days. There's no time to relocate him."

"I don't understand. How can I help?"

"El Tigre likes to return to the scene of his body dumps. It's a vanity thing. His way of telling us that he can be anywhere or do anything he wants. In the past, he's come back to leave some tiny scrap of evidence that links back to the murder. It's nothing we can ever use to find him, he's much too clever for that. Just enough for us to know that he revisited the body's dump site."

"Like what?" I ask.

"In the past, he's taken the victim's ID, then returned it to the scene of the crime. Another time he returned a ring. Completely clean of prints. Things like that."

"Sounds creepy."

"It's rather brilliant, actually," says Billings with a hint of admiration in her voice. "What we want is for you to keep an eye out for anyone suspicious. Can you do that for us?"

"I'd love to, except Agent Parks, or was it Rollins—anyhoo, one of them told me we had to keep The Bistro closed until further notice. If the place is closed, then how is this El Tigre going to come back here without raising suspicion?"

"I can override that closing. If you agree to help us, The Bistro can open up Monday morning right on schedule. We'll install some out-of-sight cameras that will be manned twenty-four seven. You'll be completely safe."

If we can open up Monday as usual, we won't lose revenue. Which takes a bit of the sting out of losing the *Battle of the Beach Eats* gig.

"What if I don't agree?"

She shrugs. "Then we might have to keep The Bistro closed indefinitely. Or at least until we tie up all the loose ends, which might take weeks. Who knows?"

"That's blackmail."

"It's called cooperating with a federal agency and helping your country."

She's got me there. "Okay, sure. I'll help. What if I see someone acting funny, what do I do then?"

"You immediately call Fontaine here. He'll be our liaison. And if you remember anything, anything at all that stands out, then report that too. Anything, no matter how small or trivial could be important."

"I guess I could do that. What about my partner Sarah? Shouldn't we tell her what's going on?"

"Absolutely not. The only reason I'm bringing you in on this is because you're already aware of the situation. The fewer people who know, the better." She gets up to leave. "Another thing." She makes a disgusted face. "Apparently, Joey has a thing for your double chocolate chip muffins. He's requested I bring some back with me."

"Sure, I can do that." I try not to sound as ridiculously pleased as I feel. Double chocolate chip is my favorite too.

She shoots Travis a parting look. "You get Joey's muffins. I'll meet you in the car."

I barely wait until she's out of earshot. "Boy, she's intense. So what happened to 'I know nothing, I'll say nothing, and I'll do nothing.'"

"What happened is that the Bureau needs your help," he says tightly.

"Looks like you need it too." Gloating isn't a good look, but I can't help myself.

Travis glances between Paco and me. "I admit, at first I thought the bit about the dog finding the dead body was crazy, but this makes three dead bodies now."

"I told you. Paco has skills."

"You expect me to believe that he's a ghost whisperer?"

"I think you already do."

"Let's say I buy it. What else am I missing here?" He spears me with an intense gaze. It's almost like he can see right through me. For one horrible second, I wonder if Jim told Travis about my gift. But no, Jim wouldn't do that. He promised me he wouldn't tell anyone, and I believe him.

"You're not missing anything," I say. We go down to the kitchen where I put a half dozen muffins, five of the double chocolate chip, and one orange cranberry (in case Joey needs a bit of variety), into a bag, then hand it to Travis.

"You're not staying here tonight, are you?" he asks.

"Why not?"

"Someone literally dumped a dead body in your back yard. I'd feel a lot better if you stayed with your brother or your parents."

"Well, I wouldn't. I like my own bed just fine, thanks. Now if you don't mind, I'm having dinner with my family tonight and I'm already late." I make a shooing motion with my hand.

"You're the most stubborn ... Okay. But don't forget to—"

"I know, I know. Lock the door behind you."

Chapter Nine

I CAN'T GET THE look on Travis's face out of my head. I know that Jim would never reveal my secret to him, but something tells me that Travis is on to me. Or at the very least, on some level, he knows something about me is off.

I also can't stop obsessing about El Tigre. To think, a world-famous hitman has been in my café and I didn't even know it. He probably walked right into The Bistro, ordered coffee and a muffin, and I'm sure I smiled at him because I smile at all my customers.

I wonder what kind of muffin he ordered. And if he liked it. Oh no. I hope he didn't come in the day that I put too much flour in the lemon poppy seed muffins. They came out a bit too doughy and ...

Not important, Lucy!

After a quick shower, I head over to my parents. The house smells of my mom's chicken cacciatore causing my stomach to rumble in anticipation. Paco does a happy dance. "Remember," I warn him as we go through the front door, "we're on our best behavior which means no begging."

He barks in response.

I'm no sooner in the door than my entire family, Will included, descend on me like a flock of wild egrets. News of the dead guy has gotten around town, which was to be expected eventually, but I thought I'd have time to tell them first.

"We just heard what happened at The Bistro," says Will. "Why didn't you call and tell us?"

"Sorry, my bad. It just happened this afternoon. I didn't think it would get around this fast."

"What is going on here?" Mom demands. "How did a dead body get into your parking lot?"

Why does everyone think I had any control over this?

"Technically, it was in the dumpster."

Dad makes a pained face. "Does this have anything to do with ... you know, your gift?"

"You mean her ability to sniff out a lie?" Sebastian clarifies.

Mom tsks. "I have no idea where she got that." She glares at Dad. "It must come from your side of the family."

I guess this isn't a good time to tell them that Paco sees ghosts.

"I think you should stay here at your parents' house tonight," says Will.

"You and Travis both, but I don't see why."

"*Why*?" Will mimics. "Because some psycho has used your place to dump a dead body! Who knows where this killer is now?"

I'd forgotten that no one except me and a handful of cops are privy to the whole Joey "The Weasel" situation. If they knew this was all mob related, then they'd know that I'm safe. Sort of. I mean, no one's getting a half million dollars to whack me, so what would be the point?

As if things couldn't get worse, the front doorbell rings, and it's Brittany.

I'm pretty sure Brittany has only been to my parents' home twice. Once back when I was seven and Mom made me invite the whole class to my birthday party, and some other random time back in fifth grade when we were in the same Girl Scout troop. She greets everyone with her dazzling Brittany smile. "I'm sorry to interrupt, but I need to speak to Lucy."

"We were just going to sit down to dinner," says Mom. "George, put an extra plate on the table."

"Oh! That's so sweet of you, but I couldn't intrude."

"Any friend of Lucy's is always welcome for dinner."

Brittany glances shyly at Will. "If you're absolutely certain ..."

"We insist! Right, Lucy?"

"Right," I say, although I have a feeling I'm going to regret this.

"We were just scolding Lucy here for not telling us about what happened at The Bistro this afternoon," Dad says.

"Oh! It was horrible. I was there too."

Mom puts an arm around Brittany to console her. "Do the police have any clue who the dead man was, or what he was doing there to begin with?"

"They're still investigating," I say vaguely.

"It was probably some tourist," Dad says. "Each season they get weirder and weirder."

"So, what did you need to see me about?" I ask Brittany.

"Just to tell you that ... that *thing* I was looking into doesn't appear too promising right now."

Which means Brittany hasn't found any dirt on Catfish Cove. Which means, we should pretty much kiss *Battle of the Beach Eats* goodbye. Not that I'd held out any real hope.

A timer goes off in the kitchen. Mom calls us all to dinner, and we migrate to the dining room table. Paco settles on the floor at my feet, and begins to chew on a bone.

Mom passes around the salad. "I only have one rule at my dinner table. No politics."

Dad grins. "I guess that just leaves religion."

"Speaking of which, I heard at the Piggly Wiggly that Mrs. O'Donnell got doused during the nine-a.m. mass last week." Mom looks to Sebastian for confirmation.

He groans. "The church roof is leaking." St. Perpetua's Catholic Church, where my brother is pastor, is ancient. The roof has been leaking for years, but last Sunday it rained buckets, bringing the situation to crisis status.

"Can't the bishop do anything about it?" asks Mom.

"The diocese is willing to help, but we have to raise at least half the money ourselves."

"Which means you need to get your sermon on," Will says.

Sebastian makes a face. My brother gives wonderful sermons, but he hates asking for money, and I don't blame him.

"You can count on your mother and me to contribute our fair share."

"And I can give you a dollar fifty," I joke. Which isn't funny at all because that's about how much I'll have in my checking account after I pay this month's bills.

"What's the status on that Cooking Channel show?" asks Will.

"Zip," I say.

Brittany glances around the table. "I'm afraid that Whispering Bay is currently out of the running due to that incident at The Bistro today."

"But that's not anyone's fault," says Sebastian.

"Oh, I agree, but, unfortunately, Tara Bell, that's the producer in charge of the show, and her cameraman were at The Bistro when Lucy discovered the body. I think the notoriety associated with that might be too much."

Even though Brittany has worded that carefully, there's still a tiny thread of implication that somehow this is all my fault. As if I had any control over this El Tigre person!

Dad scowls. "So, the cops have no clue who this dead guy was, or who might have done this?"

"Nope," I say, then rush to add, "But even if they did, I'm not sure they'd tell me. I mean, why would they?" Then I do this thing that I hate. I laugh snort. It's something I do when I get nervous like I am right now because I hate lying to my family, but if they knew I was going to be helping the Bureau catch a notorious hitman, they'd probably lock me up in my old room and throw away the key.

Time to change the subject.

"I can't believe how quickly the two of you put the house back together," I say, glancing around the dining room "It's like you never left."

"If you lived here then you could watch the place while we were gone," Mom says. "A young unmarried girl like yourself. No reason you can't live with your parents. We aren't even here half the year!"

This is a point my mom likes to make whenever she can. My dad backs her up by nodding.

"I love living over The Bistro in my own place."

"Even after that horrible woman nearly killed you in the kitchen?" Mom asks incredulously. "And now this dead body in your trash bin?"

"How about we amend that rule to no discussing politics *or* dead bodies?" I semi-joke.

There's a moment's awkward silence.

I give Will a look that says I need help here.

"Yeah, so, how was book club?" Will asks.

Yikes. Maybe we should go back to talking about dead bodies.

"Lucy got kicked out her first night," says Dad. "Betty Jean Collins was at The Bistro yesterday telling everyone who would listen how Lucy never showed up and how she let everyone down because they were really counting on her muffins for the refreshments."

Will looks surprised. "I thought you were looking forward to dissecting this new J.R. Quicksilver novel. What happened?"

"It's J. W., not J.R.," Mom corrects teasingly. "Will! You're a librarian. You should know things like that." She leans eagerly in my direction. "Was Betty Jean's book club discussing *Assassin's Honor*? I loved that book!"

My mom has read *Assassin's Honor*?

"I planned to go to book club," I say to Will. "But ... I had to stay at the café to receive an important delivery, and I got busy and forgot to call Betty Jean."

"I certainly hope she doesn't ask *me* to join her book club," Mom says. "Not after kicking out my own flesh and blood. Still, I wonder how the rest of the group liked the book. I'm sure there were some lively discussions."

"This one is J.W.'s best," says Dad. "*Assassin's Creed* used to be my favorite, but he outdid himself with this latest."

Dad has read *Assassin's Honor* too?

Ew! Chapter fourteen is totally ruined for me now.

Sebastian takes a sip of his wine. "This book sounds very popular. Maybe I should read it too."

"No!" We all shout at the same time.

"Lots of violence," says Dad, shaking his head. "Disgusting, really. You wouldn't like it. You wouldn't like it at all."

Sebastian raises an amused brow. He turns to Will. "What did you think of the book?"

"You know Will doesn't read popular fiction," I say. "He's too high brow for that."

"I'm sure Lucy means that in a very nice way," Mom interjects.

"No offense taken," says Will.

Mom perks up like she's just remembered something. "Sebastian tells me that the Young Catholic Singles are going up to Atlanta to attend a football game next weekend. Sounds like fun, doesn't it?"

I nearly choke on a piece of chicken. Young Catholic Singles is exactly what the name implies—it's a bunch of desperate twenty-and-thirty-somethings who haven't been able to find anyone on whatever online dating site is popular at the moment. I wouldn't know since I refuse to use one. Plus, I just don't have the time.

Will catches my eye.

Sebastian coughs into his napkin.

And Brittany says, "Oh, but, Lucy doesn't—"

"Know if she's going yet!" I interrupt giving Brittany a look that says *shut up*!

Miraculously, Brittany, who's usually clueless with nonverbal communication, gets the hint and snaps her trap.

"Well, you should," says Mom, "and when you get to Atlanta call your aunt Doreen."

"Why would I do that?" I ask more out of curiosity than anything else, because I have no intention of going on this field trip.

"To say hello, naturally, since you'll both be in the same city."

I bite my tongue. Mom and dad were in their late thirties before they started having children. They're not that old, and they both certainly know how to use a cell phone, but Mom still thinks that calling long distance will incur charges.

"I probably won't be going to Atlanta," I say carefully.

"Why not?"

Because I'm not a member of Young Catholic Singles.

"Because even though it doesn't look good right now, there's still a super slim chance that the Cooking Channel might pick us for their show. I need to be available whenever they want to start filming. Right?" I say to Brittany, hoping she'll back me up.

"Oh, yes! Lucy's right," she jumps in. "It looks rather bleak, but the situation isn't totally hopeless."

Since this makes sense, Mom doesn't argue. "How about you, Will? Are you going?"

"Actually, I haven't gone to any of the meetings lately."

"*What*? Why not? Oh, Will, you have to go! A young, handsome single man like you? It's a shame that you're not putting yourself out there. Isn't it, George?" She elbows my father.

"Molly, leave the kids alone."

"When I was Lucy's age, I used to love going to Young Catholic Singles. It's how I met your father and look how that turned out!"

"Nowadays they have Tinder," says Dad.

"Tinder?" Mom frowns. "What's that?"

"It's like Uber," I say, "except instead of getting a ride you get a hookup."

Will snorts.

"I think it's sad that both Lucy and Will don't have anyone in their lives," Mom muses. "I can't remember the last time Lucy went out on a date."

Good thing my Mom is back in town to make me feel special.

To be fair, it isn't just me she's picking at.

"When was the last time you took out a nice girl?" she demands of Will. If this were any other person sitting at our table, Mom would never put them on the spot like this, but since Will is like a second son to her, she has no shame grilling him the same way she does me.

Sebastian grins. "As opposed to a not nice girl?"

"Be quiet, you," Mom warns. "Well?" she persists.

Will looks as uncomfortable as we all feel right now.

"What about you, Brittany?" Mom asks. "Surely you have to be seeing someone."

Brittany delicately lays down her napkin. "Will took me to dinner last week."

Mom's face lights up. "What! Why didn't you say so? George, did you hear? Will and Brittany are dating!"

"I'm not deaf, Molly." Dad gives them both a pitying look.

Will clears his throat. "It was just one date. But we had a nice time. Um, didn't we?"

"Oh, yes! We had a great time!" Brittany says, beaming at Will.

Huh. Brittany is telling the truth. At least, in her view, the date was a success.

"There you go!" Mom slaps her hands together like it's a done deal. "Now we just have to find someone for Lucy."

I can't stand this anymore. Before I can stop myself, I say, "I'm kind of seeing someone too."

Everyone at the table turns to look at me, including Will. "I thought you said you weren't going to go out with Travis."

"Travis? Who is this Travis?" Mom asks. "Is he Catholic?" Travis could be a homeless drug addict, but Mom focuses on what's important.

"Yep," says Sebastian. "Catholic and a cop. From Dallas. His dad just retired here, and Travis moved to be closer to him."

"Oh! He sounds wonderful!"

"I never said I was going out with Travis. It's ... someone else."

"What?" Brittany looks as if she's just had her favorite tube of lip gloss stolen. "How come I didn't know this before? I thought I was your best friend!"

Rats. Now everyone is staring at me and—

My cell phone pings.

"Lucy, you know I don't want those things at the table," scolds Mom.

"Sorry, but I'm on alert in case the cops need to come by The Bistro again to collect evidence." Hey, it could be true.

My phone pings again.

"You might as well answer that," Dad says.

I pick it up and glance at the screen to see a text.

You said Sundays were your day off. Want to grab some brunch tomorrow?

The texter's area code isn't local.

Who is this??? I text back.

Sorry. It's Mike Armandi. Rocko gave me your number. I hope that's okay.

"Is it the cops?" asks Will.

"No, it's Mike Armandi. He wants to know if I'm free for brunch tomorrow."

"Who's Mike Armandi?" asks Dad.

"He's ... the guy I'm dating."

Sebastian frowns. "The guy who made the deliveries the other morning at The Bistro?"

"That's the one."

Mom mulls this over. "He seemed very Italian."

"He is," I assure them. "Big family. His uncle is a sweetheart. We have absolutely *lots* in common."

"Like what?" Will asks.

"Well, we both like to eat. He's crazy about my pumpkin spice muffins."

"Everyone's crazy about your pumpkin spice muffins," Sebastian says dismissively.

Will's forehead scrunches up making him look adorable. "How come you never mentioned him before?"

"Haven't I? I guess with all that's been going on, I just forgot."

What are the odds that Mike Armandi would ask me out at the same exact moment I needed it? This is like some weird and wonderful Kismet. Like the universe just reached out to hand me this little gift.

Do I want to go to brunch with Mike Armandi?

Why not?

He's pleasant enough. And if I go on this one date, I can truthfully say I've gone out with him and I won't be lying anymore. Besides, if I turn him down the universe might think I'm ungrateful.

I text him back. **Sounds good. Where and when?**

The Harbor House. Pick you up at 11?

It's a date!

I put my phone down. "We're going out to brunch tomorrow. The Harbor House," I add casually.

No one says anything, and thankfully, a couple of minutes later, the conversation goes back to St. Perpetua's leaky roof. But every once in a while, I catch Will looking at me with a strange expression on his face.

Chapter Ten

AFTER DINNER, BRITTANY HELPS mom and me clear the table while the men do the dishes. Since tomorrow is Sunday which is Sebastian's big day of the week, he leaves immediately afterward to practice his homily. Poor guy. He's already sweating having to ask the congregation to cough up the money for the church roof.

Brittany leaves soon after, and Will and I play cards with my parents for an hour or so before we call it a night.

Paco and I are out the door and almost to my car when Will catches up to me. "I'm following you home."

"No need to, I'm—"

"I'm not asking permission. I'm telling you."

"Oh all right."

Whatever. Will can follow me if he wants to. I'm not about to argue with him knowing that El Tigre is out there somewhere. I know he doesn't want to hurt me, but if Agent Billings is right, then El Tigre is planning to make a repeat visit to The Bistro to leave his trademark clue. I'm really not looking forward to that.

It didn't seem like such a big deal during the daytime, but it's after ten and pitch-black outside. Because The Bistro back parking lot faces the gulf, we can't keep artificial lights on otherwise it confuses the baby sea turtles. The motion detector light above the kitchen door doesn't seem like enough protection anymore.

So, yeah, I'm glad Will followed me.

I unlock the kitchen door and turn on the lights. "Want to—"

"Yep," he says brushing his way past me. "Did you record last night's episode of *America's Most Vicious Criminals?*"

"Naturally."

Even though we both had double helpings of chicken cacciatore, we still stuff ourselves with popcorn while we watch the recording. The episode, featuring a double homicide that took place on board a yacht, is especially gruesome.

"Why do people use knives?" I ask. "I mean, all that stabbing and blood. Yuck."

"You prefer your murder less messy?" Will teases.

I think about Ken Cameron and Mark Rinaldi and how little blood there actually was. One small bullet hole between the eyes and bam! I shudder.

"What's wrong?"

"Nothing," I say, still thinking about what I've seen this week. El Tigre might be a ruthless killer, but I don't think his victims suffered before they died. So, there's that at least.

We watch all the way to the previews at the end. I get up and stretch, expecting Will to take off, but instead, he goes to my linen closet and pulls out a blanket and a pillow.

"I'm sleeping on your couch tonight," he announces. "End of story."

Will is sleeping on my living room couch, a fact I'm hyper-aware of because I can't get to sleep. The man I've been lusting after for the past nineteen years (well, technically, it's only been the last ten that lust was involved) is lying less than twenty feet away from me and the only thing separating us is a paper-thin wall and the sad fact that he only thinks of me as a friend.

Sometime in the night, I fall asleep. I know this because I semi-wake up in the middle of a horrible dream. At least, I think it's a dream. And for sure it was horrible because someone was trying to break into my kitchen. Paco was doing his psycho barking and—

Paco's wet nose nudges me fully awake.

He barks, runs around my bed in a circle, then jumps down, urging me with his eyes to follow him.

I dash out of bed and into the living room.

"Will, wake up!"

Paco reinforces this with more urgent barking.

Will shoots off my couch like it's on fire. He's barefoot but other than that he's still wearing all his clothes, which is unfortunate. Living in a beach town, I've had the privilege of seeing Will without a shirt on lots of times. But it never gets old. Let's just say it's up there with coffee, chocolate, and Netflix.

Focus, Lucy.

"What time is it?" he asks wild-eyed. Before I can answer, he looks down at his watch. "Lucy, it's two in the morning!"

"There's someone in the parking lot."

He freezes. "Are you sure?"

"Yes, I'm sure. Something woke me up. Paco hears it too."

Paco is still barking, only now he's doing this little dance where he's basically chasing his tail. Not sure what that means, but I've never seen him do this before. The one thing I am sure of is that he's trying to tell me something, and that something isn't good.

"I'll go take a look," Will says. "You stay up here. Call the cops."

Of course I'm going to call the cops, but there's no way I'm going to stay up here cowering in my apartment while Will plays caveman and checks this out on his own.

I'm about to dial 911 when it occurs to me. This could be El Tigre. Which means I have to keep this on the low down. Or the down low. Whichever.

I follow Agent Billings instructions and dial Travis.

He answers on the first ring.

"I'm on my way," he says before I can even say anything, which I have to admit is reassuring. I hang up and follow Will down the stairs. It's dark and eerily quiet. He turns on the dining room light but hesitates in front of the door that leads into the kitchen.

"What exactly did you hear?" he whispers.

"Footsteps in the parking lot, maybe? I'm not sure."

Will blinks the sleep from his eyes. "You heard footsteps in the parking lot while you were upstairs? What do you have? Bionic ears?"

I roll my eyes. "I know I heard something." Paco nudges me with his nose again. Now that we've come downstairs to investigate, he isn't barking anymore. He's glued to my side, but whether he's trying to protect me, or he wants me to protect him, I'm not sure. Either way, I'm glad he's here.

Will slowly opens the door. He flips on the kitchen light. Everything is exactly the way I left it.

We look at each other in relief.

The door that leads to the back parking lot is firmly closed with no signs of a break in.

Then I hear the noise again.

Will turns to look at me. Oh God. This isn't the result of eating too much popcorn last night. I read an article that said carb overload could make you hallucinate. If that's the case, then I'm in deep doo-doo because the only thing I love more than muffins is bread, but this isn't my imagination because Will hears it too.

He walks toward the door like he's going to open it and see what's out there.

"Will, hold on. We should wait till the cops get here."

"I'm just going to take a quick look around the parking lot."

Will has no idea of the potential danger out there. He doesn't know anything about the FBI or the mob or El Tigre. He's like an innocent lamb being led to the slaughter. No way am I about to let that happen.

I grab the heaviest frying pan I can find. Ironically, it's the same one used to whack me on the head just a week ago. Good. Having personal experience with this thing I can testify it makes a friggin' good weapon.

"No," I say firmly. "You absolutely cannot open that door. I won't let you."

Will looks startled by the vehemence in my voice. Of the two of us, I'm the one who usually jumps over the cliff with no thought of what lies below.

"Lucy, do you know something I don't know?"

"Actually ... yes."

Will frowns. "Go on."

I know I'm not supposed to tell anyone about El Tigre, but I have to. It's the only way to keep Will safe.

"Okay, so—"

There's a loud knock on the door startling us both. I'd recognize that knock anywhere. "It's Travis. Let him in."

Will opens the door.

Travis takes one look at him, barefoot with his hair rumpled, then his gaze shoots over to me. I'm wearing my pink fleece Pac-Man pajama pants and my sweatshirt that says MUFFINS ARE NOT UGLY CUPCAKES. I'm also barefoot, and my hair has probably made a trip to crazy town and back. It must look like the two of us have just ...

My face goes hot.

Will ushers Travis into the kitchen. "Glad to see you, man."

Travis, I notice also looks like he's just woken up. He's wearing sweatpants and a T-shirt and no socks with his sneakers. It makes me feel a whole lot safer knowing that he literally flew out of bed when I called. He's also got a gun, which I'm not a big fan of, but in this case, *yes, please.*

"What's going on?" he asks.

"Will and I both heard a noise outside in the parking lot."

"I notified the team on my way over," says Travis. "They should be here in ten minutes or less."

"Team?" Will says, confused.

Travis doesn't miss a beat. "Since there was a dead body found in the dumpster here yesterday, we have to assume this could be related."

Will nods. "Have they identified the body yet?"

"I think I hear a car now," Travis says, smoothly avoiding Will's question. Travis catches my gaze, but his expression is guarded. "You two stay here." He closes the door firmly behind him.

I run to the front of the café and look out the window. Two dark-colored sedans roll into the parking lot. Agent Billings, followed by the rest of her team, swarm the premises.

"Looks like I better put on some coffee."

Two hours later the FBI team is gone. Will offers to take Paco for a walk, leaving Travis and me alone in the kitchen.

"You didn't find anything?" Not that I want them to find anything, but … *Correction*: I would have been ecstatic if they'd found El Tigre and this whole thing had been resolved. Even though there's no one around to hear, I lower my voice. "Not even his signature trademark?"

"Nothing."

"Sorry to have woken you up. But, I could have sworn I heard something."

"You were right to call. No worries."

"I hate that I got you out of bed for nothing."

"It's my job. I told you, right now I'm on call twenty-four seven until this is resolved."

"Well … thank you."

I catch him staring at my sweatshirt. A corner of his mouth twitches like he's trying not to laugh. His gaze slowly goes down to my pink pajama bottoms. "Pac-Man? Isn't that kind of old school?"

"It's making a resurgence."

He doesn't say anything. Which makes me nervous.

"So, really, thank you. I wish I could make it up to you." I glance around my kitchen. "How about I make you breakfast? I know you think I just make muffins but—"

And then it happens.

Out of nowhere, well, not completely out of nowhere, because my Spidey sense warned me this would happen sooner or later, Travis kisses me.

He cups the back of my head in his big hand, leans down and softly covers my mouth with his. I admit, it's rather lovely.

I haven't kissed a lot of guys before, but I can tell he knows what he's doing. Patient, but not too patient, because just when I begin to feel restless, he urges my mouth open and I get just the tiniest hint of tongue action before he pulls away. Leaving me wanting more.

The cad.

This, of course, is an excellent reminder of why I shouldn't get involved with Travis Fontaine. He's much too smooth for me. Plus, I'm in love with Will. So, there's that.

I try to act very cool and sophisticated like the kiss didn't affect me at all.

"Let me know when you're ready for more of that," he says like he can see right through my act.

I cross my arms over my chest. "You're completely shameless."

"In what way?" he asks, amused.

"I'm ... sleeping with another man, and you just waltz into my kitchen and kiss me!"

"What? You mean Cunningham?" He frowns. "That's not the vibe I'm getting."

"Then your vibe-meter is wrong."

"No, it isn't," he says smugly.

Before I can respond to that outrageous statement, the door opens, and Will and Paco come in from their walk. "Hey," Will says oblivious to what's just happened, "anyone want breakfast? I'll cook."

"Travis can't stay," I blurt. "He just got another call he needs to respond to. But I'd love breakfast, thank you."

At first, Travis doesn't say anything and for one terrible second, I think he's going to out our kiss to Will, but then he says, "Sorry to miss breakfast." He gives me a meaningful look on his way out the door. "Call me if anything else happens."

Will waits until Travis is gone. "You okay? You look flushed."

"It's no wonder after all that's happened tonight."

"You sure that's it? Did Travis find something out there?"

"No, nothing." I do not want to talk about Travis anymore, so I fake a big smile. "What about that breakfast you promised?"

Will makes pancakes and bacon. I fill up Paco's bowl with his dog food, and the three of us sit around in the kitchen, Will and me on stools at the counter, and Paco at our feet.

Will waits till my brain is lulled by all the food to say, "I hope this doesn't ruin your brunch with Mike this morning."

Mike who?

Mike Armandi! I'd completely forgotten all about him.

It's official. I am now a ho.

Will just spent the night.

Less than an hour ago, Travis kissed me.

And in … I check the kitchen clock, less than six hours I have a brunch date with Mike.

Okay, so Will didn't spend the night in the Biblical sense, which means I'm just a PG-rated ho. But still, three men in less than twelve hours. That has to be a record. At least, it is for me.

"Tell me about this Mike guy," Will urges.

I shrug, trying to act nonchalant. "He's just a nice guy who delivers our supplies."

"And the two of you are going out, huh?"

If I didn't know better, I'd think Will was jealous.

"It's a first date," I confess. "We might not get along. We'll see."

"What's going on, Lucy?"

"What do you mean?"

"You seem on edge."

"*Hello*! Dead body in my dumpster? Remember? You're the one who insisted on spending the night to protect me, which, in hindsight was an excellent idea." Because even though Travis says they didn't find anything, I still have the niggling suspicion that someone was out in the parking lot.

"I've known you almost all your life. You're hiding something from me. What is it?"

"What do you mean? I'm not hiding anything."

"Bull."

The irony of this moment isn't lost on me. Will is the only person I've never caught in a lie. He's also the hardest person on the planet to read. Apparently, though, he can see right through me. I feel like I'm in that dream where you're naked and everyone is staring at you.

"Before Travis showed up, you were going to tell me something important."

True, but that's because Will was so adamant on checking out the parking lot and I thought El Tigre was out there.

"So, what was it?" he persists.

I can't tell him about El Tigre, but I can tell him about Paco. "If I tell you, you'll laugh."

"I would never laugh at you, Lucy."

"Paco sees dead people."

Will starts chuckling.

"I'm going to slap you."

"I thought we already went through this."

When I first found out that Paco's former name was Cornelius and that the Sunshine Ghost Society thought he was a ghost whisperer, I had the same reaction. But three dead bodies have changed my mind.

"Yesterday, when I went to take out the trash, Paco already knew there was a dead body inside the dumpster."

"Of course he did. Dogs have a keen sense of smell."

"But he led to me to straight to Abby!" I say, referencing our first dead body together.

"Paco was in the rec center when Abby was murdered. He led you to her because he's a smart dog. Nothing more." He gentles his voice. "He doesn't see ghosts. Okay?"

I'm itching to tell Will how Paco found Ken Cameron's body. Sure, he's right about Abby and maybe about dumpster guy, but jumping out a car window and leading me to a dead body through an empty soccer field is no coincidence. Only I can't tell Will about any of that because I promised Travis to keep it under wraps. Plus, it would probably get me in trouble with the FBI.

"Prove it," I say.

"Prove what?"

"Prove to me that Paco can't see ghosts."

"You can't prove a negative." He clicks his tongue and Paco trots over. "Hey, boy," he croons, scratching him behind the ears. Paco falls at Will's feet. Not that I blame him. "He's just a dog, Lucy. He doesn't have any kind of special powers."

If I could tell him about Ken Cameron, then he'd believe me, but I can't, so I'll just have to keep my mouth shut.

Chapter Eleven

By the time we're done with our early breakfast it's past six, so Will goes back to his place. Since today is Sunday and my brother is a priest I can't very well skip church, so after I get ready for my big "date" with Mike, I go to nine a.m. mass. Luckily, it's a clear day, so nobody gets soaked during my brother's oh-so-uncomfortable sermon where he asks for money to repair the roof on St. Perpetua's.

Poor Sebastian. He looks as if he's about to pass out while imploring us to open our hearts and wallets so that everyone can stay dry.

My parents are at mass. So are Jim and Travis Fontaine.

Everyone notices that I'm a bit more dressed up than usual.

"Lucy!" Mom says, "You look wonderful!" I'm wearing mascara and blush and yes, lipstick. I tossed half my closet onto my bed trying to decide what to wear for this brunch. I've always been a T-shirt and jeans girl. Extra points for comfy sneakers, so anything other than a simple skirt and flats is a challenge for me.

In the end, I selected a flowery dress that I wore to my cousin's outdoor wedding a few years ago. It's nice but not too dressy, and paired with a light blue sweater and wedge heels, I don't think I'll embarrass myself.

Despite that I'm wearing heels, Travis still towers over me. "You look nice," he says with just an edge of something in his voice that makes my insides go all gooey.

No. I refuse to be this weak.

"Thanks." I introduce Travis and his dad to my parents. They all shake hands and make polite small talk.

"So, Travis, are you a member of Young Catholic Singles?" Mom asks, making me cringe. Geez. The way Mom is pushing this group, it's like she gets a kickback for every member she recruits.

Travis clears his throat. "No, ma'am, I'm not. I've been pretty busy at work since moving here."

"We've heard," Dad says, shaking his head. "I have no idea what's going on in this town. It used to be Whispering Bay was the safest city in America. Not anymore."

Travis and I exchange a look. If Dad only knew what was *really* going on. Even after the events of the past few days I still can't wrap my head around it. According to Agent Billings, this El Tigre could be anywhere. Maybe he's even here at church. I discreetly watch as people dip their fingers into the holy water and make the sign of the cross on their way out the door, but all I see are familiar faces.

"Are you going to the parish hall for coffee and doughnuts?" Jim asks us.

"George and I never miss the doughnuts," says Mom, "But Lucy needs to go meet her new boyfriend. His name is Mike ... what's his last name again? It's something Italian. Maybe Travis can run a background check on him."

"Lucy has a new boyfriend?" Travis's green eyes glitter with amusement. "I'd be happy to run a background check. What's his name? I'll need his date of birth, too."

If I could only kick him ...

"It's no big deal," I say. "Just a first date."

"Where are you going?" Travis asks.

As if I'd tell him.

I glance at my wristwatch. "Oops! Have to dash. Bye, all!" I scurry away before this turns into the Monty Python version of the Spanish Inquisition.

I drive back to The Bistro, put Paco on his leash, and take him for a quick walk. We get back just in time to see a red pickup truck with New Jersey license plates pull into the parking lot.

Mike is wearing jeans and a nice blue button-down shirt. "What's with all the yellow tape?"

Pretty much everyone in town knows all about the dead body in the dumpster, but Mike isn't from Whispering Bay, so I feel free to fill him in on what happened.

He whistles low under his breath. "Did you see anything? I mean, do you have any idea who the guy was, or who might have done it?"

"Nope," I lie since I'm not at liberty to discuss this with anyone. "Totally clueless here."

"I've never been this close to a crime scene," Mike says. "Do you mind showing me where you found the body?"

The hairs on my neck feel as if they've been plugged into an electric socket. This isn't Mike's first rodeo when it comes to crime scenes. He's seen a dead body before too. I can sense it as clearly as I know my own name. But why lie about it?

I should tell him the area is off-limits, but I'm curious to see if he's going to lie again. "As long as we don't touch anything, it should be okay."

We go under the yellow tape and I show him the dumpster. He takes his time, scrutinizing the scene as he walks around.

"Must have been pretty scary, huh? Are you okay?" Then before I can answer, he says, "Sorry, that's a dumb question."

My Spidey sense tells me his concern is real.

"I'm okay, but yeah, I was pretty shaken up most of yesterday."

"How long will The Bistro be closed? Should I cancel this week's order? Rocko won't mind. We can reschedule whenever."

"Actually, we're reopening tomorrow."

He looks surprised. "That's fast."

Paco barks at Mike to get his attention. "Cute dog. What's his name?"

"Paco."

"Hey, Paco." Mike crouches down to pet him. "Didn't mean to ignore you, little fella." Paco allows himself to be petted, then he jumps into the open door of Mike's truck and stubbornly plants himself in the front seat. He's giving me his *I'm going, and you can't stop me* look.

Mike laughs. "Looks like your dog wants to come along."

"Paco, get down from there this instant," I say using my firm voice.

He ignores me and stares straight ahead. He's never openly defied me before. What's going on here?

"Paco. Did you hear me? I don't need a chaperone."

Mike laughs again like he's finding the whole situation cute, but frankly, it's annoying. I mean, I love the little guy, but I don't want him tagging along on my date.

"The Harbor House has an outdoor patio that faces the ocean. I checked it out when I made a delivery there the other day. I'm pretty sure they allow dogs. I don't mind if he comes, if you don't."

Paco turns to look at me with an expression that can only be described as smug.

I shouldn't let him get away with this, but then his eyes go all big and soft on me, and like the chump I am, I give in. "Okay. Just this one time."

Mike's cell goes off. "Do you mind if I take this?"

"Sure, go ahead. I'll wait for you in the truck."

He turns his back to me to take the call in private.

I get into the front seat and Paco plops himself down onto my lap smearing dirt onto my flowery dress. *Rats*. He must have stepped into some mud during our walk. I check my bag to see if I have anything to wipe the dirt off with. Nope. Maybe Mike keeps paper towels in his glove compartment. I pop it open. There's no wipes or towels, just a few manuals, and a ... *gun*?

I swallow hard.

Mike keeps a gun in the glove compartment of his pickup truck.

I know a few people who own handguns for protection and plenty who own shotguns for hunting, so it shouldn't surprise me, but I'm still staring at it when he comes back from his call.

"Ready to go?" He follows my gaze.

"Oh! Um, sorry, I wasn't snooping." I gesture to the mud stain on my dress. "I was hoping to find something to wipe this off with."

"No worries." He calmly reaches across and shuts the glove compartment, then pulls out a clean towel from a gym bag in the back seat. "Here, this should help."

"Thanks." I manage to get off most of the dirt. The small bit that's left blends into the floral pattern of my dress, so it doesn't look too bad.

"I have a permit for that gun, by the way. In case you're wondering."

"I wasn't, but now that you mention it ..." I laugh snort. "I guess driving a delivery truck can be dangerous?"

"So I've been told." He smiles but it feels forced. "Ready for some brunch?"

The Harbor House's parking lot is full of expensive sports cars, but Mike doesn't seem fazed. He hands the keys to his slightly dented pickup truck to one of the pimply faced valets and the three of us head into the foyer.

"What a cute dog!" The hostess smiles at Paco. "I'm sorry, but we only allow animals in our outdoor seating section," she tells us.

"Perfect," says Mike.

She leads us outside to the patio and low and behold who is sitting at the outdoor bar nursing a beer? Man Bun. Minus Tara, thank goodness because I just don't think I can put up with her kind of energy right now.

Man Bun looks up from his drink. "Hey."

"Oh, hi ..." I search my brain for his real name— "Wade! No, I'm sorry, it's Wayne. Right?"

"How's it going?" he drawls.

I introduce him to Mike. The two men shake hands. "Wayne works for the Cooking Channel. He was part of the film crew that was at The Bistro when we found that, *um*, surprise in the dumpster."

"All that work for nothing," Man Bun (because that's the only way I can think of him) says glumly. "The cops swiped all our film. They say they're not giving it back either."

"What are you still doing in town?" I ask.

He hesitates a fraction of a second before saying, "Waiting to hear about my next assignment."

An odd tingle runs down my spine making my Spidey sense sit up straight. This isn't exactly a lie, but he's hiding something. Something big. Something he doesn't want anyone to know.

"If we could continue this way, please?" The hostess says trying to guide us toward our table.

"Nice seeing you, Wayne," I say.

He mumbles something that sounds like *you too*.

We get a table facing the water. Paco, I'm happy to say, is now behaving perfectly. He lays next to my feet and watches the customers and wait staff with an eagle eye. It's almost as if he's looking out for me, like a little bodyguard. I can't be irritated with him anymore, because, how cute is that?

"So, this is a nice break, huh?" Mike says after our drinks arrive.

I nod and take a sip of my mimosa. He's right. Working in the restaurant business, it's always nice to be on the other side of the table for a change.

"How long have you worked for Rocko?" I ask trying to make conversation. Other than the crime scene lie, Mike seems like a nice enough guy, and this date has only been going on for half an hour, but I can already tell there's no fizz between us. No chemistry. No gooey feeling in the pit of my stomach like when Travis kissed me ...

Nope. Not gonna think about that.

I'm pretty sure Mike feels the same way because he shifts around in his chair like he's uncomfortable. Or maybe he's just feeling a bit squished. He really is a big guy.

"I've been doing Rocko's route for about a week now."

"Oh." I assumed he'd worked for Rocko longer. "Where did you work before that?"

He shrugs. "Here and there."

Not exactly a lie, but evasive enough that it makes me curious.

"But you've driven a delivery truck before?"

"Not really." He clears his throat. "Tell me more about your job. Must be fun making cupcakes all day."

I stifle a moan. "Muffins," I clarify. "There's a big difference."

"Sure, sure," he says quickly. "Nice being your own boss though, huh?"

"Yes, but it can be stressful too."

"Like how?" He leans forward in his chair like he's interested, only I know it's not me he's interested in.

"Well, you're responsible for everything, and then there's the long hours and the feeling that you're always behind. And you never really leave work because you're always thinking about it. That's one of the reasons Sarah and I decided to close one day a week. We wanted to make sure we didn't get burned out."

"Yeah," he muses, "I guess there's all that."

The server brings us our food. We're about to dig in when I hear a familiar voice shouting my name across the room.

"Lucy! Thank God, I've found you!" Without an introduction or even another word, Brittany plops herself down in the empty seat across from me.

"Oh, hi, Brittany. This is—"

"Brittany Kelly, Lucy's best friend." She reaches across the table to shake Mike's hand. "You must be Lucy's new boyfriend. I'm soooo glad to meet you!"

If only the earth could swallow me whole right now. But I'm not that lucky.

Mike looks confused. "Boyfriend? Oh, I um ..."

"Brittany is mixing you up with someone else. So sorry." I try to catch Brittany's eye, but her nonverbal communication skills have really gone down the sink today.

"Aren't you the produce supplier?" she asks.

"Kind of," he says. "I'm filling in for my Uncle Rocko for a few weeks."

"So, you're *not* Lucy's new boyfriend?"

"Brittany!" I say with a chuckle like this is all some great big misunderstanding. "What are you doing here?"

"This is my Daddy's restaurant. I'm always here. Well, at mealtimes, anyway."

"I mean what are you doing here right now?"

"Looking for you, silly. I need you to come with me right away and convince Tara not to leave town. Did you see Wade in the bar? Or is his name Wayne? Whatever it is, I told the manager to give him anything he wants, on the house."

"I thought we were out of the running for *Battle of the Beach Eats*."

"Until it's formally announced that they're picking Catfish Cove over us, then hope is still alive. You don't think I'm going to let something as trivial as a dead body in The Bistro parking lot stop me, do you?"

The couple sitting at the next table turn to look at us. They begin to whisper.

"Keep your voice down," I hiss. "And it was the dumpster, not the parking lot."

"Whatever." She pulls at my arm trying to get me to leave.

"But I haven't finished my shrimp and scallop omelet yet!"

"Is food all you can think about right now?"

"Maybe we should try this some other time?" Mike says to me.

"Good idea," says Brittany. "I'll make sure Lucy gets home."

Mike mumbles an awkward goodbye and leaves some cash on the table before heading out.

I toss my napkin on the table. "Do you know how rude that was?"

She blinks back a tear. "I'm sorry. I just can't lose this opportunity with the Cooking Channel. The Chamber of Commerce is depending on me."

"What exactly do you want me to do?"

"I want you to apologize to Tara."

"*Apologize*? What for? I didn't do anything."

"Lucy, the dead body was found in *your* restaurant dumpster. Those horrible state CSI people harassed Tara then stole the film from Wade's camera. Maybe technically it wasn't your fault, but..." She shrugs.

As ridiculous as this sounds, Brittany is right. We can't afford to let an opportunity like the Cooking Channel slip away. "Okay, okay, I'll talk to Tara, although I have no idea what I'm going to say to her or how it might help."

The server comes by to see if we need anything. "Oh, Miss Kelly, I didn't know you were here. Can I get you something?"

"No need, Phil," Brittany says with a brilliant smile. "Will you please put the tab on the family account?" She points to the cash Mike left on the table. "You can keep that as a tip."

"Thanks!"

I'm about to ask the server to box up my uneaten omelet but before I can do that Brittany begins snapping off orders again. "Let's go. We don't have a second to waste." She notices Paco at my feet. "Oh! Hello, baby!" Paco wags his tail furiously in response.

Clearly, Brittany isn't going to leave me alone until I do exactly what she says. "I need to go to the bathroom first. Meet you up front."

Brittany leaves to get her car from the valet. Since I'm not supposed to take Paco inside the restaurant, we head toward the outdoor bathroom area. There's only one stall and it's unisex. I hope there isn't a line. I go around the side of the building, but Paco lunges ahead of me causing me to drop his leash.

"Paco! What are you doing?"

I spy him running toward the sandy area behind the restaurant. I hope he isn't chasing a seagull or some poor helpless turtle. This part of the beach isn't dog-friendly. The last thing I need on my plate right now is a ticket, so I chase after him, but I'm not used to running in wedge heels. After a few wobbly steps, I stop to take off my shoes. When I look up, he's gone.

What in the world?

A cold fizzy feeling washes over me. The only time Paco acts like this is when …

No. This can't be happening. I'm going to think positive here. He might be a ghost whisperer, but he's also a dog, and dogs get distracted by lots of things. I look toward the shoreline and squint, but I don't see him.

I trace my steps back to the building. The area outside the bathroom stall is quiet. The door is ajar.

A whimpering sound from inside makes me freeze.

"Paco?"

The whimpering gets louder.

I put my hand on the doorknob to open it all the way when I hear my name again. "There you are!" says Brittany. "I've been waiting for you for over five minutes! Haven't you gone to the bathroom yet?"

I whirl around. "I ... I was about to," I manage to say.

She scowls. "Lucy, we don't have all day." Before I can stop her, she flings back the bathroom door.

The first thing I see is Paco, sitting there patiently looking up at me like he's saying, *It's about time you showed up.*

Then my gaze moves to the dead body crumpled on the ground. It's a man. Mid-forties, bald. And he's got a bullet right between his eyes.

Chapter Twelve

"WHERE AM I?" BRITTANY whimpers.

I press a wet paper towel against her forehead. "Are you okay? No, don't move. You might have hurt yourself when you fainted. I called 911."

"I fainted?" she asks in a daze. She tries to turn her head so she can look around.

"Stay still. If you get up too fast, you might get woozy again." I don't want her to get another glimpse of the dead guy lying just a couple of feet away. Not until there's someone else here to back me up, because I'm pretty sure she'll either:

A. Scream.

B. Pass out again.

C. Do something else equally as dramatic.

Because let's face it, she's Brittany.

Not that I'd blame her if she did any of the above. It's not every day you come face to face with a mob hit. And that's exactly what this is. I should know. This is my third one in the last four days. Even Paco seems to be accustomed to the M.O.

Because she's Brittany, she does exactly the opposite of what I tell her to. She turns her head and looks straight into the dead guy's face, screams, and scrambles as far away from the body as possible.

At least she didn't pass out again.

Brittany's screaming causes a crowd to gather around the open stall door. A man who identifies himself as the restaurant manager, pushes his way through. He takes a look at the dead guy, and for one horrible second, I think he's going to pass out too. Then he recognizes Brittany.

"Miss Kelly!" He puts a protective arm around her even though I'm pretty sure she's safe from the guy on the floor. We all are.

Now the cops and the ambulance have arrived. One of the paramedics examines Brittany. Zeke takes one look at me and sighs. "Lucy," he says, shaking his head.

"Not my fault that my dog is gifted when it comes to sniffing out corpses."

Zeke looks at Paco who wags his tail as if he agrees with me.

It seems like half the Whispering Bay Police Department is here. Including Travis.

Billings and the suits arrive, pretending to be part of the state's super-elite CSI team and it's a repeat of the other day all over again, only thank goodness this time it's not happening at my café. Now there's yellow tape all around The Harbor House too. I do my best to answer all of their questions. The way Agent Billings glares at me, you'd think I'm a suspect.

The paramedics satisfy themselves that Brittany doesn't need to go to the hospital, so now it's the police and the FBI's turn to question her.

I find Travis alone for a second and take the opportunity to see if I can get any info from him. "Have they identified the guy in the stall yet?"

"Where's your date?"

"Does that mean you aren't going to tell me?" I ask in a mockingly sweet voice. "Remember, I'm supposed to be helping the Bureau here." Then to answer his question. "My date left early."

"How early?"

"About fifteen minutes before Paco and I found the body."

"So he missed all the action, huh? We still need to question him." He hands me that irritating notebook he writes everything down in. "His name and number, please."

"Are you going to tell me who that is in the bathroom? I already know it's not some random customer."

"Take a guess."

"He doesn't have that clean-cut FBI look about him, so I'd say he was another hitman on his way to kill Joey. Only El Tigre got to him first."

"I'd say that was a pretty good guess." Travis gets called away by one of the suits. "We'll talk later."

I'm about to call my parents to reassure them I'm okay, when I spot Brittany. She still looks dazed. Her eyes are puffy and her cheeks are wet. Her mascara, however, still looks perfect. Go, Brittany!

"Are you okay?"

She nods woodenly. "How about you?"

"I'm okay too."

"Oh, Lucy! It was so horrible! I don't think I'm ever going to get over this."

And because I can't help myself, I hug her.

"I'll probably have to go to counseling," she says, sniffling.

"Yes, of course. Counseling sounds like a wonderful idea. Very beneficial."

"And—" Brittany's cell phone rings. "Hold that thought." She pulls her phone out. "Yes? Oh! Tara! How are you? What? No ... no, Tara, I beg you! This is all going to blow over. Yes, of *course*, I promise. Whispering Bay is still the wholesome beach town you're looking for. We might not be America's safest city anymore, but we're definitely America's most interesting one!" She gives a weak little laugh. There's a pause. "I see. Yes, I understand." She clicks off.

"I'm sorry, Brittany. You tried your best. No one can blame you for any of—"

"Sorry for what?" she snaps.

"I take it that Tara has already heard about this most recent dead body?"

"Wade probably couldn't wait to call her," she fumes. "I should cut off his bar tab."

"Does that mean we're definitely out of the running for *Battle of the Beach Eats*?"

"The network wants to make a decision by the end of the week. If we can keep any more dead bodies from surfacing then maybe we can reclaim our image. It's a slim chance, but there's still hope."

"How exactly are we supposed to keep more dead bodies from surfacing?"

"I don't know, Lucy," she says sarcastically. "Maybe you can stop being an enabler and make sure Zeke Grant and the rest of the police department actually do their job instead of hanging around The Bistro all day drinking coffee and eating muffins."

"Hey! Zeke only comes in the morning and—"

"Speaking of Zeke Grant. There he is! I'm simply going to have to insist the police do something about these dead bodies. They're ruining all my plans." She takes off on her mission with a brisk pace.

And just like that, Brittany is back.

Just when it looks like things are wrapping up, Agent Billings take me off to the side. "We need to speak in private."

She ushers Paco and me to an empty office room inside the restaurant. A minute later, Travis joins us. "I'll let Fontaine explain the situation."

"The guy in the stall was Eddie O'Leary," he begins.

"Better known to his associates as The Hatchet," she finishes.

The Hatchet? And here I thought El Tigre sounded scary. I really don't want to know how this O'Leary character got his nickname, although I've seen the movie *Scarface* so I can imagine.

"You have my complete attention."

"We're going to install secret cameras both inside and outside The Bistro this afternoon. When your place opens back up tomorrow and El Tigre makes his move, we'll have him on film."

"What if he's scoping out the place and sees you putting in the cameras? Won't he know to avoid coming back?"

She smiles smugly. "I told you, El Tigre thinks he's invincible. He'll probably welcome the extra challenge of the cameras. It's never stopped him before, but this time it's different. We're counting on you to point out any customers that stand out. Anyone who isn't a regular. He's never worked a small town like this. He's been able to avoid detection in places like New York or Miami or Moscow because of the crowds. But here in Whispering Bay? I feel confident that this time we'll be able to nab him."

"Are you going to be installing cameras here at The Harbor House? I mean, he'll be back here too, won't he? To leave his trademark clue?"

"If he continues with his pattern, which, he will, then yes, but there's no time to place surveillance equipment in both establishments. Your café is much smaller. It will be easier to concentrate our efforts in one spot."

"What about last night? Are you sure there wasn't anyone in my parking lot? Maybe El Tigre already left his clue. Because I did hear something. My dog heard it too."

"Positive. We're professionals. If someone had been there, we would have found something." She narrows her eyes at me. "I don't know what's going on here, but I'm not a fool. It's no coincidence that you're the one who's found all the dead bodies. I'm too busy trying to keep Joey alive right now, but when this is all over, I'm going to want some answers. Got it, McGuffin?"

"Sure, I got it."

"Good." She nods to Travis. "I'm going to wrap it up out there. You can give McGuffin a ride home. Make sure she understands that we're not playing around here. Rollins!" she screeches on her way out the door. "Have you printed everyone yet?"

Argh. This woman ...

"So do you believe me now?" I ask Travis. "Are you going to admit that Paco is a ghost whisperer?"

"You're right. He did lead you to those dead bodies. There's no other explanation."

Wait. *What*? That was way too easy.

"Are you hosing me?"

"Absolutely not." He studies Paco. "You don't know much about his origins, do you?"

"I know he belonged to Susan Van Dyke and that she used to have séances in her home, and that he participated." I wrinkle my nose in distaste. "And that his name used to be Cornelius."

"But before then?"

According to Paco's history, Susan found him wandering down the street, with no collar. "I don't know anything about him before Susan."

"Exactly. He could be a highly specialized police or military dog trained to search for cadavers."

"If he's that specially trained, why wasn't he wearing a collar? Or why hasn't some agency come looking for him?"

"Maybe they have. As soon as I have time, I'm going to look into this."

Travis can look into this all he wants, but he's not going to find anything. Paco is a ghost whisperer. End of story.

"You ready to go home now?" Travis guides us through the side door to the restaurant where a police car is waiting.

"Too bad your boyfriend wasn't here when all this happened," he says dryly. "Oh, wait. You have two of them, right? The one you're sleeping with and the one you were here having brunch with?"

Travis is having way too much fun at my expense. "Can I ride in the front with you?"

"No, you have to ride in the back. Preferably handcuffed."

I can't help but crack a smile. I settle Paco in the back (unhand-cuffed) and strap myself into the front seat. "Can I play with the radio?"

"What are you? Ten?"

"Twenty-six. And Mike Armandi isn't my boyfriend. We were just having brunch. And you know perfectly well that I'm not sleeping with Will. We're just friends."

He looks at me sideways. "But you want it to be more, right?"

My stomach sinks. It's not fair to flirt with Travis and put him off at the same time. I need to be honest with him and lay all my cards on the table. "Yes, but it's all one-sided."

"Are you sure about that? You should tell him, Lucy. Maybe Will feels the same way you do. Maybe he doesn't. But until you ask, you're never going to find out. And until then, you and I can't happen."

"You and I? I don't get it. Every girl in this town is after you. Why me?"

"Hell if I know. But are you going to sit there and tell me you didn't like it when I kissed you last night?"

Rats. I wish I could honestly say no. But I can't.

"I liked it. Some."

He grins. "Liar. You liked it a lot. I did too." He starts the engine. "Tell Will how you feel. And when you figure it all out, let me know."

Chapter Thirteen

Paco and I go back to The Bistro where, good to her word, Agent Billings' FBI crew is already there installing cameras. They're dressed in T-shirts that advertise some bogus refrigeration company so that anyone driving by would assume that we're getting repair work done.

Except El Tigre will know something's up. According to Agent Billings, he won't care. Instead, he'll consider it a challenge. I can't wait until this is all over and my life gets back to normal again.

As if my life could ever go back to normal anyway.

You should tell him, Lucy. Maybe Will feels the same way you do. Maybe he doesn't. But until you ask, you're never going to find out, and until then, you and I can't happen.

Tell Will how I feel about him?

Easy for Travis to say. He's not the one who could potentially lose his best friend forever.

I try to ignore the undercover crew and do the same thing I do every other Sunday afternoon. I go over the business's emails, which is super boring but maybe it will take my mind off Will and Travis and this whole FBI business.

Sarah is really good about checking our account every morning so she can stay on top of things. Anything that's important, she flags so that I'll make sure to read it.

I make myself a cup of coffee and settle down in front of my laptop. The first thing that catches my attention is an email from Rocko: *Sorry I've missed the last few deliveries. This broken leg is messing me up bad. I hope my brother Jimmy has been keeping up with the orders. Should be back to my usual route in a few weeks. Meanwhile, if you need anything, just let me know. I'll make sure Jimmy keeps you stocked.*

Broken leg? I thought Mike said Rocko was on vacation.

And who the heck is Jimmy? Rocko's brother Tony used to run our route until Rocko took over. I've never heard of this Jimmy before.

I look for earlier emails in the thread, but I don't see any.

I pick up my phone and dial Sarah.

"Lucy! I heard about what happened at The Harbor House. Are you okay? What on earth is going on? Do you think these two murders are connected? I mean, they have to be. Right?"

I wish I could tell Sarah the truth. Of all the people I've lied to since this started, she's the one that bothers me most. The Bistro is half hers. She should know what's going on. Tomorrow morning when we open up and start serving customers, she'll be oblivious to what's going on, while I, on the other hand, will be on the lookout for a ruthless professional hitman capable of taking out anyone who stands in his way. I'm already a nervous wreck. But if I tell Sarah, then I could get in big trouble with the FBI, plus I could potentially put her in danger, and that's the last thing I want.

"It's crazy, huh? Say, Sarah, when Rocko's nephew came in the other day to bring us our order, you said you already knew about it from Rocko?"

"Yeah, he emailed to tell me he'd been in the hospital and that his brother would be taking over his route. I meant to keep it, for reference, but I accidentally deleted it. Sorry."

"Did he give a specific name for this brother?"

"Someone named Jimmy, I think?"

"So, you didn't think it was weird that this Mike guy showed up?"

"I figured he was just filling in. Why? What's wrong?"

"Nothing's wrong. I just ... wanted to update our supply list, and I want to make sure to email it to the right person. I'm trying out a new muffin recipe and I need pecans."

"Just email Rocko at the usual address. He'll take care of it. Isn't it great that the cops are letting us open tomorrow?"

"Yeah, great," I say woodenly before we say our goodbyes and hang up.

The wheels in my head begin to spin. This whole thing with Rocko seems off. Before I lose my nerve, I email him back: *Hope you're feeling better! I want to add pecans to our bi-weekly delivery. See the amount below. And one more thing. Jimmy hasn't been making the deliveries. Your nephew Mike is doing the route. Should I expect him to continue?*

I hit send then wait a few minutes. No reply. I'm sure Rocko has better things to do than sit around his computer waiting to answer my emails.

I pace around the room. Then I take off my flowery dress and get into some comfy jeans and a sweatshirt. Next on my list is a call to my parents to fill them in on what happened at The Harbor House so they don't flip out. *Guess what*? They flip out anyway. I do my best to reassure them that despite having found another dead body, I'm doing just fine.

I get off the phone and check my computer again.

Still no reply from Rocko. He probably won't answer till tomorrow—

A pinging sound tells me that my email server has just refreshed. I have a new message from Rocko!

Thanks, Lucy. I'm getting better every day. I'll add pecans to your list. Can't wait to hear what kind of muffins you'll be making with those. Sorry about the delivery confusion. Mike is Jimmy's son. He wasn't scheduled to make deliveries on your route. He can be a little rough. Hope he did okay. I'll make sure Jimmy takes care of you from now on.

Mmmm ...

I scan the email again.

Rocko is trying to be professional, but I can certainly read between the lines. He had no idea that his nephew was making our deliveries.

I've caught Mike in two lies now. The first time was when he said Rocko was taking a vacation (ha!) and the second time is when he said he'd never been near a crime scene.

Hey, we all have our secrets.

"You're not planning to kill anyone, are you?" I tease.

"Not today."

My heart nearly explodes from my chest.

Holy wow.

I think I've just found El Tigre.

Chapter Fourteen

I TALK MYSELF THROUGH it one more time.

Fact: Mike knows his way around The Bistro including the kitchen and the parking lot. When I think of how eager he was to take out our trash! It should have been a big fat red flag. I mean, how many delivery guys offer to take out your trash?

Zilch.

Fact: He lied to me about never having been around a crime scene. Ha! According to Agent Billings, El Tigre practically wrote the crime scene handbook.

Fact: He had plenty of time to whack Eddie "The Hatchet", stuff the body in the bathroom, and have the valet bring him his truck all before Paco discovered what he'd done.

To think, there I was sipping on a mimosa trying to make small talk with a man who doesn't even know the difference between a muffin and a cupcake. I should have known then he was a sociopath.

Fact: Agent Billings said El Tigre was from New York. Mike is from New Jersey. Same thing.

Fact: Mike keeps a gun in his glove compartment!

How much more evidence do I need?

My blood begins to boil. Here I thought he was flirting with me when all this time he was scoping out my café for one of his body dump sites.

Well, he's not going to get away with it. Not any of it.

Paco and I head straight to Will's place.

He looks surprised to see me. "I thought you were on a date with this Mike guy."

I walk in and plop down on one of his leather sofas. "I was, but luckily I escaped with my life."

"Sounds like the date from hell."

"You have no idea."

No use in beating around the bush. "Paco found another dead body in the outdoor bathroom at The Harbor House. And before you say it's all a great big coincidence, this makes the *fourth* body he's found, which makes it statistically impossible. So, see? He really is a ghost whisperer."

Will collapses on the sofa next to me. "Four?"

"Before we begin, promise me you won't tell Travis that I told you any of this. Or anyone else either."

"What are we? Back in grade school?"

"This is really important, Will."

"Okay, I promise."

"I didn't miss book club because of an after-hours delivery to The Bistro like I told everyone. I missed book club because on the way to Betty Jean's house, Paco jumped out the car window."

"While you were driving?"

"I'd just rolled to a stop."

"He's not hurt, is he?" Will picks Paco up and runs his hands down his back to reassure himself that he's okay.

"No, thank God."

"Why would he do something crazy like that?"

"He jumped out the car window and made me chase him down an empty soccer field near the city park. Where he led me to a dead guy, who'd been shot between the eyes."

"A dead body? In the park?" Will takes a few seconds to absorb this. "Why hasn't this come out in the news?"

"This is the part you really can't tell anyone, or the two of us might end up in Sing Sing or Rikers Island. Or worse, Quantico."

"Lucy," Will says with a chuckle, "Quantico isn't a prison. It's FBI headquarters."

"Exactly. Ken Cameron, that's the name of the dead guy in the park, was an FBI agent. They probably have a secret torture room at Quantico where they take people who know too much, and I have no desire to be waterboarded, thank you."

"Seriously? An FBI agent? How do you know this?"

I tell Will everything that's happened in the past few days, including the situation with Joey Frizzone.

"This is unbelievable. Why would Travis tell you any of this? Wouldn't the FBI want to keep this strictly confidential?"

"Yes, but since I found the dead guy at the park I already knew too much, so to keep me quiet they had to fill me in. Remember the guy I followed to Dolphin Isles? He's the dead FBI agent! The one Kitty Pappas thinks is a honeymooner. At first, Travis made me promise not to get involved in any way at all. But then, after I found that dead mobster in my dumpster, Agent Billings, she's the one in charge of the whole enchilada, asked me if I could help."

"The FBI wants your help?" he says incredulously. "What do they think you can do? You bake muffins, for God's sake."

"*Hey*! I bake the world's best muffins, thank you."

"That goes without saying, but come on, Lucy. Be real. How are you supposed to find some rogue hitman—"

"His name is El Tigre."

Will grunts. "Sounds like something out of *Scarface*."

"Doesn't it?"

"My point being if the FBI can't find this guy, how are you going to do it?"

"They're installing cameras in The Bistro. Apparently, this El Tigre has some kind of signature move that involves revisiting his crime scenes to leave a clue."

He perks up with interest. "He goes back to his crime scenes?"

"It's like he's flaunting it in their faces. Which means he's coming back to The Bistro in the next couple of days. That's how they're hoping to catch him. Sarah doesn't know anything about any of this. Since I already know what's going on, they're hoping I can help identify anyone who comes back to the café that I might find suspicious."

Will stiffens. "Last night, when you didn't want me to check out the parking lot on my own, that's because you thought El Tigre was out there?"

"Sorry, I wanted to tell you, but I couldn't."

"I don't like it. I don't think the FBI should involve you in this."

"Why not?"

"Because you're a civilian!"

"You've forgotten I've already solved one of their cold cases. The Angel of Death, remember?"

"And you also almost got yourself killed in the process."

"But I didn't. Look, the FBI and the cops are getting nowhere. First, there's the agent in the park. Then there's this Mark Rinaldi in the dumpster at The Bistro, and now there's Eddie "The Hatchet" O'Leary at The Harbor House. Who knows who'll end up dead tomorrow? Obviously, they need my help. Besides, I'm pretty sure I know who El Tigre is."

"Oh yeah?" Will looks part amused, part exasperated. "Who?"

"Mike Armandi."

"Your new boyfriend?"

I wave my hand dismissively. "He's not my new boyfriend, and you know it. I only said that to get Mom out of my hair."

I tell Will all the facts, including how Rocko had no clue that Mike was doing our deliveries. "Don't you see? He must have found out that Joey, The Weasel, was in Whispering Bay and he decided to use his uncle's delivery business as a cover. Pretty brilliant if you ask me. He probably broke his own uncle's leg," I add with a shudder.

"Let's say I buy this. How did this Mike or El Tigre or whatever you want to call him know that Joey was here in Whispering Bay to begin with?"

"Probably from Ken Cameron. He must have sold Joey out to the mob."

"The dead FBI agent? Why would El Tigre kill him if Ken Cameron was selling him information?"

"Maybe Ken wanted more money. Or maybe El Tigre just wanted him out of the way so that Ken couldn't double cross him and re-locate Joey. Who knows? It could be any of a dozen reasons. When your nickname is El Tigre you don't need much of an excuse to kill someone."

"Have you told Agent Billings your theory yet?"

"No, and I don't intend to."

"Why not? Let them check it out. It's their job."

"Because right now it's just a bunch of circumstantial evidence. What gives it more credibility is the fact that I've caught Mike in two big lies."

"Ah," says Will, finally getting it.

"Yeah. I'm not about to tell Agent Billings that I'm some kind of freakish human lie detector."

Will gives me a thoughtful look. "Are you sure about those lies, Lucy?"

"Positive."

"So what are you going to do?"

"I'm going to set a trap for El Tigre and get him to confess."

Will laughs. And not in a nice way. "How exactly are you going to do that?"

"I have no idea, but considering the FBI is batting zero, I can't do much worse, can I? I figure between the two of us, we can—"

"*No.*"

"You don't even know what I'm about to say."

"Let me guess. Between the two of us, we're going to trip up some ruthless professional hitman who's determined to get a half-million-dollar bounty by killing an FBI informant. Oh, and anyone else who gets in his way too. Sure! Why not? I'm going to channel Travis here. Leave. This. To. The. Professionals."

"Believe me, I'd be happy to, but if I don't do something then the Cooking Channel is going to pick another town to host *Battle of the Beach Eats*. Which means I can't win the show and I lose the chance for twenty-five grand."

"So this is about money? Why didn't you say so? I can give you more."

"More? You've already lent me ten thousand dollars."

"I've told you. No need to pay me back. Consider it a gift."

"Absolutely not. I have to pay you back that money."

"If you feel the need to pay me back then comp me a muffin every day for the next year and we'll be even."

I refuse to even acknowledge this ridiculous suggestion.

"Man, you're stubborn," Will says.

"So are you."

We lock gazes for a few seconds before it becomes too awkward and we break away.

"How were you able to lend me so much money to begin with?" I ask. "You can't be that great a saver."

"We've been through this before. One of my aunts left me some money after she passed away."

Before Will lent me the money for my share of the down payment on The Bistro I'd never even heard of this mysterious aunt.

I take a deep breath and focus on relaxing every inch of my body in hopes that I'll get some sort of reaction. But there's none. No tingling of the little hairs. No Spidey sense screaming at me. *Nada*. Is Will telling the truth? I truly can't tell. This is one of the many times I wish my gift worked on him. Of all the people in the world to be immune to my inner lie detector, why him?

"I still need to pay you back. And nothing you can say will change my mind about that. But catching El Tigre isn't just about getting on the Cooking Channel and winning the show. This is personal. It's about taking back my town. This guy stuck a dead body in my dumpster. You think I'm going to let him get away with that?"

Will gets up and paces around the living room, then turns to look at me. "I'm going to regret this, but, okay. I don't know what you think it is I can do, but I'll help. On one condition."

"Really? Yes, anything!"

"You have to tell Travis what you're doing and how you're doing it. Otherwise, I'm out."

"You mean ... you want me to tell Travis that I'm a human lie detector? He isn't going to believe me."

"Not at first. So you'll have to prove it to him."

"But—"

"That's the only way I'm going to help you, Lucy. Because if something goes wrong with your plan, we're going to need the cops to get us out of whatever mess it is you've got cooked up."

Chapter Fifteen

WILL THINKS HE'S SO clever. He's counting that I won't tell Travis about my gift. And he would be right, because I don't share that part of myself with anyone. The only reason I told Jim Fontaine was because I sensed I could trust him and I needed his advice.

But anyone else? Nah. Not even Sarah, who I consider to be one of my best friends, knows that sniffing out lies is built into my DNA. The last thing I want is for anyone to constantly worry about what they say around me, because, let's face it, lies are an everyday occurrence. Without them, life would be difficult.

Take the other day at the dentist. When Margie, my long-time hygienist, asked me if I was still flossing twice a day, of course, I said, "Yes!" Margie and I both know that's a lie, but if I told her the truth, then she'd be obligated to give me the floss-twice-a-day speech and nobody has time for that.

Another reason I don't tell anyone about my lie detecting skills is because the last thing I want to do is stand out in a not-so-good way. I'm already not your typical twenty-six-year-old. I get up at four-thirty every morning to make muffins which means that by eight p.m. I'm passed out drooling in my bed (except for Friday nights when I stay up late to watch *America's Most Vicious Criminals*). My favorite shoes are converse sneakers. I've never had a serious boyfriend. And my dog sees ghosts.

None of which makes for a catchy Match.com profile.

Nope. I think I'll just keep my little secret to myself, thank you very much.

Will might think he has the upper hand here, but he's sadly mistaken if he assumes I'm just going to lay down and let El Tigre ruin my town. No sirree. For once, Brittany and I are on the same page. I need to prove to the Cooking Channel that Whispering Bay is the perfect location for their next season of *Battle of the Beach Eats*.

Will is right about something, though. Running off to investigate this on my own could be dangerous. My lesson with the frying pan taught me that. But there's also a sense of urgency here. I can't just sit back and wait for El Tigre to show up at The Bistro to leave his trademark piece of evidence. Who knows how many more hitmen he'll kill before then? The streets of Whispering Bay could be lined with dead bodies.

I definitely need to be on the offensive, and that begins with doing a reconnaissance of the safe house where they've stashed Joey. What I might discover, I don't know, but I need to do something.

I park my car far enough away from the neighborhood entrance that it can't be seen from any of the streets. With my new binoculars around my neck, Paco and I creep around the back entrance to the cul-de-sac. Or rather, I creep, while he marks every tree and shrub he can find. *Men.*

Since it's Sunday, children are riding their bikes along the sidewalk and adults are doing yard work. We're just a couple of weeks away from Thanksgiving, so pumpkins are everywhere. Luckily, the cul-de-sac seems quieter than the rest of the neighborhood. There's a man a few houses down from the safe house mowing his yard, but other than that there's no activity.

I wonder if Agent Billings is keeping watch through a window. Knowing her, she's probably got security cameras in place. I pull my baseball cap down over my forehead. As long as Paco and I keep behind the bushes, we should be okay. I offer him a liver treat from my pocket. He greedily gobbles it down.

"There's more where that came from," I whisper. "Be quiet and stay out of sight and you'll get one every fifteen minutes."

His eyes go bright with anticipation.

I hesitated to bring him along on this mission, but he's so smart. Besides, we're a team. If it weren't for Paco, I'd be swimming with the fishes already.

I hunker down low and take a look through the binoculars. Just like the other day, there are no cars in front of the safe house and the garage door is closed.

A movement near the street catches my attention. A minivan drives through slowly like they're checking out each house. I adjust the binoculars to see if I can get a better look at the driver.

It's a man. And ...

Rats. There's a woman next to him and two kids in the back. Probably a family scoping out the neighborhood for potential homes.

Nothing else happens for the next thirty minutes. I reach into my sweatshirt pocket and pull out another treat. I have eight left, so we should be good for a couple more hours, but by then it will be full on dark. *Note to Lucy*: Bring a flashlight the next time you do recon.

I twist around to offer Paco the treat, but instead of taking it, he leaps out from our hiding place like he's possessed. He takes off running down the street, his leash trailing behind him.

What?

I have no choice. I run after him. I try my best to snatch the end of the leash, but he's too fast. The only time Paco acts like this is when …

Oh please *no*. Not again.

I just don't think I can deal with two dead bodies on the same day.

I follow the sound of his crazy barking to the edge of a lot where a big water oak stands on the corner. Paco barks and jumps in the air like he's trying to climb after something, and that's when I see what's caused all the commotion.

A squirrel.

Ugh. I almost wish it had been a dead body because squirrels are the vilest animals alive. They're Satan's minions doing his evil bidding here on earth.

"Paco!" I grab the end of his leash and try to pull him away, but it's no use. He's determined to get that squirrel, although what he'd do with it is beyond me. Probably lick it to death.

Paco's barking becomes more violent. That's when I see that there's not just one squirrel, there's three. All snarling with their big rodent teeth plotting how they'll attack.

On an intellectual level, I know my fear of squirrels is irrational, but knowing that doesn't do me any good when my heart is beating out of my chest and my palms are going all sweaty.

I have to get out of here.

"Lucy!" A familiar voice makes me spin around.

It's Sally from the library. She's wearing jogging clothes. Her hair is green today. She still looks cute, but I liked her pink hair better.

"Are you okay?" She asks, reading the panic on my face.

I nod woodenly.

She quickly takes control of the situation. Gripping hold of Paco's leash, she uses a firm, but slightly scolding voice. "That's enough."

Miraculously, he obeys her. He continues to growl at the squirrels while Sally pulls him from his spot at the bottom of the tree, but at least he's allowing himself to be led. When we get far enough away that the squirrels aren't an issue, she hands me back the leash.

"Thanks, I suffer from—"

"Sciurophobia?" she asks.

"You know about that? Most people laugh when I tell them. They think I'm making it up."

"My brother had it too."

"Had? He's not ..."

"Dead? Oh, no! He went to a therapist who helped him get over it."

"Whew! I thought you were going to tell me he was killed by a squirrel, in which case, I would have never left the house again."

Sally laughs. "You're funny, Lucy."

"I don't know about that, but thank goodness you came by when you did. I'm not sure what I would have done."

She nods like she understands.

I've met other people with sciurophobia (there's more of us than you think), but I've never met anyone with a family member who suffered from it. Most people think squirrels are cute. But then, most people haven't been on the other end of a squirrel mob.

"I was seven when it happened," I blurt.

She doesn't say anything, so I take that as a sign to continue.

"It was my birthday party and my mom made this great cake. My whole class was there, and I was about to blow out the candles when a pack of squirrels flew out of the trees and went after my cake. So I grabbed the cake and took off running, but they chased me down. They were about to attack when Will scared them off. I know it sounds ridiculous. I know they wouldn't have really hurt me, but ..."

She places her hand on my arm. "It's okay, Lucy," she says gently. "We all have our personal demons, don't we?"

"I can't imagine you have any. You seem so put together."

"Looks can be deceiving. We all have our Achilles heel."

It occurs to me I don't know much about Sally. "Do you live around here?"

"No, my place is just a few blocks from the library, but it's such a beautiful day I thought I'd go for a jog around town."

Sally, I notice, looks like she must jog a lot. She always looks put together in her work clothes, but in her black leggings and slim fitting nylon top, she looks ultra-fit. In comparison, I'm a little embarrassed by my baggy sweat pants and my child-bearing hips.

She eyes my binoculars. "What are you doing here?"

"Oh, um, the same thing you are, except instead of jogging, I'm bird watching."

"Bird watching, huh? You probably want to leave the dog home next time."

I flush. I'm not the only one who can spot a whopper. I hope she doesn't think I'm some sort of creepy stalker.

We walk along the sidewalk, chatting, with Paco trotting between us. I wish I could go back toward the cul-de-sac, but I'm not sure how to do that without making Sally suspicious.

"How are things going with the Cooking Channel show?" she asks. "Any news yet on whether or not Whispering Bay will be selected?"

"It's looking pretty grim, especially now with this new murder at The Harbor House."

She nods sympathetically. "I heard you found the body."

I shouldn't be surprised that Sally already knows about the dead body at The Harbor House. After all, this is Whispering Bay.

"I was there eating brunch."

"With Will?"

"No, with ... someone else."

"Really? Please don't tell me you were on a date with that hunky Travis. I called dibs on him, remember?" she teases.

"Not Travis. It was someone else."

"You've surprised me, Lucy. I could have sworn ... never mind."

"What?"

She stops and looks at me. "I know I haven't been in town long, and we don't know each other all that well, but I thought you and Will had something going."

"Me and Will?" I do the laugh-snort thing. "No, no, no. We're just friends."

Sally shakes her head sadly. "Life is too short, Lucy. You should tell Will how you feel. You might just be surprised to find that he feels the same way too." Her smart watch beeps. "Oops. This thing is telling me I need to start running again." She begins jogging in place. "Let's grab some coffee soon, okay?"

Chapter Sixteen

THAT'S TWO PEOPLE IN the last twenty-four hours who have told me I need to tell Will how I feel.

I admit I was startled by how easily Sally figured out I had feelings for Will. But I can't think about that right now. I have more important matters at hand. Like how I'm going to save my town's rep and get us back in the Cooking Channel's good graces.

I stayed up half the night formulating my plot to catch El Tigre, and I've come up with the perfect solution. My plan is beautiful in its simplicity. All I have to do is get Mike to come to The Bistro (not difficult since he's doing our deliveries). We aren't due for another three days, but I'll make something up. An emergency or whatever. He will of course, jump at the chance to come here because it gives him the perfect opportunity to leave his signature clue. The feds will get it on tape and bada-bing bada-boom, he's toast.

It's brilliant. Even if I say so myself.

At exactly five a.m. I email Rocko.

Disaster! Our flour batch is filled with bugs. Is there any way you can get Mike to deliver some STAT this morning? Thanks!

There. That ought to do it.

Of course, our flour is perfectly fine, but I toss it anyway because if Mike comes and sees it, he'll immediately become suspicious, and who knows what someone named El Tigre might do if he feels cornered? I certainly don't want to find out.

Since Sarah can't know what's going on, I keep up the pretense with her as well. "Bugs? In our flour?" She makes a disgusted face. "Do you think it's a problem with the vendor or do we have an infestation in our pantry?"

Rats. I hadn't thought that far. It would be unfair to blame the vendor. And I'm not about to let poor Sarah sanitize our pantry. Not when it's already meticulously clean.

"I think it was just a freak one-time thing," I say. "It's not all bad. We had enough untainted flour that I was able to make a few dozen muffins, so we're not totally out. There should be enough muffins for our early morning customers." After all, I don't want everyone in town to suffer.

"Sorry you had to deal with that, Lucy. Hopefully, Mike will be able to work us into his delivery route this morning."

"Oh, I'm sure he will," I say confidently.

We open at seven and one by one our regular customers start filing in.

"What do you mean you're out of blueberry muffins?" asks Victor. I forgot that on Mondays he and some of his pals from the Sunshine Ghost Society come in for breakfast and talk about what sightings they've seen over the weekend. And they all love the boring blueberry. I wish I'd thought to make some of those.

"We have lemon poppy seed and pumpkin spice," I offer. I also have some double chocolate chip stashed away, in case of a muffin emergency, but this doesn't qualify.

Before Victor can tell me which kind he wants, the door opens and in walk the last two people on earth I want to see today.

Tara and Man Bun.

What are they doing here?

"Don't mind us!" Tara says, "We're here to get more footage."

Man Bun aims his camera at me. "Smile," he says like he hates his job.

"What's going on?"

"The main honchos over at the network want me to recoup the footage we lost on Saturday on the slim chance Whispering Bay gets picked up for the show. Kind of ironic, huh? We told you we'd be here Monday and here we are. Surprise! Just keep doing what you're doing. Pretend we're not here."

Victor raps his knuckles on the counter to get my attention. "My order, remember?"

"Yes, of course. So what'll it be? Lemon poppy seed or pumpkin spice?"

"Neither. I want blueberry. You always have those available."

"Sorry, we had a crisis with our flour this morning."

"What kind of crisis?" demands Phoebe Van Cleave.

"We're ... out of it."

"Out of flour?" She scowls. "Sounds like poor planning on someone's part."

"I thought I saw your delivery guy here just the other day. Just how much flour do you people use?" Victor asks. *Geez.* He's usually so easy going, but it's like I've just told him we're about to run out of oxygen or something. I had no idea how critical my blueberry muffins were to the town's ecosystem.

"I had to toss all our flour," I explain.

"Toss it? Why what was wrong with it?"

Oh boy. I probably shouldn't have said that. No way am I going to give them the same excuse I gave Rocko and tell them that I found bugs in the flour, especially when it isn't true. They might think the whole place is infested. Knowing Phoebe, she'd probably sic the health department on us. Not to mention bugs in the flour wouldn't go over well with the producers on the Cooking Channel.

I grab at the first excuse I can think of for throwing out food. "The flour was expired. Yes, that's it. Must have been a mistake with the supplier. And since here at The Bistro we're committed to using only the freshest of ingredients, we had to toss it. No flour. No muffins. Can't make muffins without the flour!"

"You're back to that old excuse, huh?" says Betty Jean. I hadn't noticed her standing in line.

Phoebe looks at me suspiciously. "How long have you people been serving food made with outdated ingredients?"

"*What*? I never said—"

"That explains the stomachache I had last week," says Victor, going pale. "I was here on three separate days and each time I had a blueberry muffin. I should have made the connection."

"Do you think the guy in the dumpster ate one of your muffins?" someone asks in a horrified voice. "Could that be what killed him?"

Oh, for the love of … It's like they've turned into a muffin mob. Clearly, I didn't think my plan all the way through.

I'm saved from responding to this ridiculousness when Rusty and Travis walk through the door. Everyone turns to shower them with questions. All of them variations of when they'll catch the mysterious "Whispering Bay Killer." If they would just wait patiently until the end of the day, they'll get their answer.

Rusty and Travis work their way to the counter.

This is the first time I've seen Travis since he gave me his unsolicited relationship advice about Will. I can't help but feel self-conscious. And even though the surveillance equipment has been in place since yesterday evening, seeing Travis and Rusty reminds me that we're being watched.

Travis glares at Tara. "What's she doing here?"

"Taking more footage."

Rusty puffs his chest out for Man Bun's camera. "Russell Newton, Whispering Bay police deputy here, placing an order." He tips his hat to me in greeting. "Hey, Lucy. We'll be needing five lattes, three breakfast sandwiches, a dozen muffins and throw in some cookies too if you have them."

"Lucy's out of muffins," says Victor.

"No, I told you, I have pumpkin spice and lemon poppy seed."

"Just give us whatever you have," says Travis.

Betty Jean growls at him. "I'll take whatever you have."

Travis chuckles. Even though he's only been in a town a few weeks, he's getting used to Betty Jean's form of flirtation.

"Not sure I'd take those muffins if I were you," Victor says, "they're made with bad flour."

Travis frowns. "What?"

I blow out a frustrated breath. "The flour is perfectly good. I just ... threw out some expired flour is all. I never baked anything with it."

At that exact same moment, Sarah comes out the door that adjoins the kitchen and the dining area and overhears what I've just said. "I thought you said the reason you threw out the flour is because there were bugs in it."

Everyone within hearing distance stills.

Sarah's face goes red as she realizes what she's just revealed.

"Bugs!" Betty Jean makes a gagging sound.

"No, no bugs," Sarah says, quickly backtracking. "I was talking about something else. My bad!" She catches my gaze and winces in apology.

"Nice try," says Phoebe, "but it's not gonna work." She gathers Victor and the other members of her group. "C'mon let's go find somewhere else to eat breakfast."

"Let us know when you get the place cleaned up," Victor yells on his way out the door. "And next time, make sure you have blueberry muffins!"

"What was that all about?" Travis asks suspiciously.

"You know the Sunshine Ghost Society." I twirl my finger around in a circle next to my ear making the universal crazy sign. I'm not sure Travis buys it, though.

"Are there really bugs in your flour?" Tara asks. Man Bun zeroes his camera in for a close up of my face. "Because we have another show you might qualify for. It's called *Dirtiest Kitchens in America.* Don't let the name put you off. There's no such thing as bad publicity! You'd be surprised how many people will still want to come and eat here. Especially if you win."

"There are absolutely *no* bugs in our flour," I announce firmly.

I get Rusty's order ready, and since I know they're Joey's favorite, I toss in a couple of the double chocolate chip muffins from my secret stash.

"See anything unusual this morning?" Travis asks in a low voice as I hand him the bag.

"Not yet, but I'm expecting things to look up soon."

"Why don't I like the sound of that?"

"Don't worry. I have everything under control."

He scowls. "Now I'm really worried. What are you up to?"

"Let's just say I have a feeling that by the end of the day, all will be revealed."

The next couple of hours go by at a snail's pace. Good thing this is Jill's day off because there's barely enough business to keep Sarah and me busy. I hope Victor and his gang haven't been running around town spreading rumors about my muffins.

By ten o'clock, there's still no sign of Mike and his delivery truck. Even though business has been slow, I've sold all our muffins, including the double chocolate chip I had on reserve. I probably shouldn't have been so hasty tossing out all that flour, but I thought Mike would have been here by now. I practically declared a state of emergency in my email to Rocko. What do I have to say to these people to get them to bring me my flour?

I'm about to give Rocko a call when Brittany shows up. But instead of freaking out because Tara is here filming, she seems perfectly poised, like she was expecting this.

"Tara!" Brittany smiles and waves to her.

"Act like we're not here!" Tara shouts from across the room.

Brittany does a double take of the dining area. "Where is everyone? It's usually packed this time of day."

"Yeah, well, we're out of muffins."

"What? How can you be out of muffins?"

Man Bun lays down his camera. "It's on account of the bugs in the flour."

Brittany's jaw drops.

"How many times do I have to say this. There are *no* bugs in the flour!"

Brittany marches around the counter and pulls me off to the side. "Lucy, what's going on? Do you know how hard I worked to get Tara interested in Whispering Bay again? Do not blow this for me. Do something! This place is like a tomb."

"Don't worry. Everything is fine." Only it isn't. Nothing is working out according to my big plan. And Brittany is right. The Bistro looks sad and empty. We look like losers. "I have an idea."

I make a phone call to Will at the library.

"What's up?" he answers.

"I need you to come to The Bistro and order something and eat it in the dining area. And ... bring some friends. Call Sebastian and anyone else who you think might come."

"Why? What's wrong?"

"Just do it. Please. The sooner the better."

Will sighs. "Okay."

It's times like this when I'm grateful to have Will for a best friend. Within an hour The Bistro is packed. Will brings over half the library staff, including Sally. Sebastian is here too, along with the receptionist from St. Perpetua's. Mom has brought her entire bridge club, and Dad's golf league just walked through the door.

Sarah and I fill orders as fast as we can. We have to call Jill to come in extra. Even Brittany has pitched in. She's got on an apron, and she's running around the dining area refilling everyone's coffee. I know it's because she's trying to make a good impression on Tara, but it's still nice of her to help.

I head down the hallway that leads to the pantry to grab some more supplies when I run into Sally, which is odd because this area is off limits to customers.

She looks flustered. "I just realized I've been here at least half a dozen times and I've never gone to the restroom. Can you point me in the right direction?"

Ouch! The little hairs on my neck feel like they've been electrocuted. Sally has definitely been to the bathroom here before, but why on earth would she lie about it? It seems silly to lie about something so benign. Maybe she's one of those persons who have no sense of direction and she's embarrassed to admit it.

"You're not the first person to get lost. It's on the other side of the dining area, next to the dolphin mural."

"Thanks, Lucy!"

I get the supplies from the pantry and am about to restock under the counter when I spot the big Armandi's delivery truck pull into our parking lot.

My heart starts thumping wildly.

It's officially show time.

Chapter
Seventeen

SARAH TAKES OVER AT the counter so I can run back to the kitchen to greet Mike. I wave from the door and motion for him to park along the back.

He brings in a pallet filled with flour. "Hey, Lucy," he says, all friendly. It's disgusting how a person can be so evil yet seem so innocent. But I can't let on how I really feel about him.

"Boy, am I glad to see you."

"Sorry I couldn't get here earlier, but I had to work you in. I had a pretty big route this morning. Rocko says you got bugs in your flour?" He heaves two big bags up on my counter. "He feels lousy about it. Called the supplier first thing this morning and chewed him out."

Uh-oh. After this is over, I'm going to have to send an apology letter to our supplier. I should probably send along a dozen of my apple walnut cream cheese muffins too. That always seems to make everyone happy.

Paco runs into the kitchen, takes one look at Mike and wiggles up to him practically begging to be petted. "Hey, pooch." Mike crouches down to scratch him behind the ears. Paco responds by licking his face.

If only Paco could see into Mike's dark soul. I thought my dog was more intuitive than this. Apparently, Paco's skills only work on dead people.

"I appreciate you coming over," I say carefully.

"Not a problem." He refills our pantry with more of the flour bags that he pulls out from the delivery truck. I turn my back, pretending like I'm busy to give him plenty of opportunity to wander over to the dumpster to leave his signature clue.

When he's done stacking the flour, he offers me the invoice. The words NO CHARGE are stamped in big red letters at the bottom of the paper, but I can't sign this, because of course, this isn't the supplier's fault.

"We need to redo this invoice. We insist on paying for the flour."

"The invoice stays as is. Rocko says he'll shoot me if you don't sign."

Oh boy. The whole family is deranged.

"Do you have time for a cup of coffee?" I ask trying to keep my voice from shaking. When I came up with this plan it seemed so simple, but I didn't think about the fact that I was going to have to be alone with El Tigre in my kitchen. I need to calm my nerves and act natural.

"Thanks, I'd love one. I haven't taken my lunch break so I got some time to kill."

Yeah, among other things.

"How about a sandwich? Turkey okay?"

"I don't want to put you to any trouble."

"No trouble at all. Sarah and I appreciate you making a special trip."

He takes the food and sits on a stool by the counter. "I'm glad I got this chance to see you. I heard things got a little crazy after I left The Harbor House."

I'll say.

"You heard about the dead body in the bathroom?"

He nods. "It was in the Panama City papers."

The skin on the back of my neck erupts into goosebumps. Mike didn't find out about Eddie "The Hatchet" O'Leary getting whacked from any newspaper. He knew about it firsthand.

"Paco and I were the ones who found the body."

He looks up from his sandwich. "Yeah, I heard about that too."

"You did?"

"The cops came to ask me a few questions." He looks at me.

"Um, yeah, when they questioned me they asked who else had been at my table, so I gave them your name." I pause. "I hope it didn't freak you out, seeing a bunch of cops at your door."

Mike snorts. "Not likely."

He's a cool one, all right. He probably thinks himself soooo above the local cops.

"You know, this murder at The Harbor House appears similar to the murder of the guy I found in the dumpster."

Mike doesn't say anything. Instead, he takes a bite of his sandwich.

"It's kind of creepy, isn't it?" I persist, trying to get a rise out of him. "We were at The Harbor House eating brunch when some poor guy was getting killed in the bathroom. It's like I don't even know what's going on in Whispering Bay anymore."

"It's scary, all right."

"You didn't see anything when you went to get your truck, did you?"

"Nope." He continues to munch on his sandwich.

We're getting nowhere here.

"So how much longer do you think you'll be doing deliveries? Rocko said he broke his leg. How bad is it?"

"Bad enough to keep him from driving for at least a couple more months."

Aha! I caught him. "Funny. I thought you told me he was on vacation." Let's see how El Tigre lies his way out of this one.

Mike lays down his sandwich. "Yeah, about that ... I said that because I felt bad, on account of I was the one who gave Rocko the broken leg."

"You did?"

"He was in my way." He shrugs.

Oh my God. Mike broke Rocko's leg? Why? Because he needed a cover and his uncle wouldn't go along?

I've got all the evidence I need.

I look around the kitchen counter.

Where's my cell phone? I need to call Travis so I can get him and the feds over here ASAP.

I spy my phone next to the refrigerator and slowly inch my way toward it. I need to keep El Tigre talking so he doesn't notice.

"Good thing you were there to fill in for him. Doing deliveries, I mean." I've got the phone in my hands now. I tap on the screen and discreetly text 911 to Travis. That should work.

"Yeah, about that. I won't be doing any more deliveries here, Lucy."

"You won't?"

"Nah. This was just temporary. I needed something less stressful than my usual job. I just have one last assignment to wrap up, then I'm outta here."

I gulp. I know exactly what that one last "assignment" is.

"So I'm afraid this is goodbye. It was nice meeting you, Lucy." He gets up to leave. Oh my God. He's on his way to kill Joey. I have to stop him.

"Hold on!"

Mike looks startled. "What?"

"You can't go just yet. You haven't … had a cookie! You can't leave without dessert. It's the most important part of the meal."

He grins. "You want to give me a cookie?"

"Well, I'd offer you a muffin, but we're all out."

Brittany waltzes into the kitchen. "Lucy, what are you doing in here?" She spots Mike and frowns. "This isn't the time to be making nookie with your boyfriend. Sarah needs your help out there."

Mike is about to open his mouth when Tara and Man Bun come up behind Brittany. "Just keep doing what you're doing!" Tara says. "We want you to act natural and real."

Just then, the door leading to the parking lot is kicked open. Travis stands there, flanked by Agent Billings on one side and Agent Rollins on the other. Or is it Agent Parks? Never mind. The important thing is that all three of them have guns. And they're pointed at Mike.

"Don't move!" says Agent Billings. "Everyone, hands in the air!"

Mike looks shocked, but he does what he's told.

Holy wow. That was easy. I thought El Tigre would put up more of a fight.

Agent Billings points her gun at Tara and Man Bun. "You too. Hands in the air."

Man Bun throws his hands up and in the process drops his camera. It falls on the tile floor with a loud shatter. "I swear, I only smoke it medicinally."

"Wade! What kind of idiot are you?" Tara screeches. "Do you know how much that camera cost?"

"For the last time, my name is Wayne!"

Tara looks as shocked as Mike. "When did you change your name to Wayne?"

"What's happening?" Brittany whimpers but nobody has time to answer her question right now.

"Are you okay?" Travis asks me.

That's him," I say pointing to Mike. "He's El Tigre. He practically admitted it to me just now."

Mike looks shocked. What an actor. "El what?"

Agent Billings keeps her gun aimed at Mike's head. "Rollins, frisk him." She cocks her head at Tara and Man Bun. "Fontaine, keep an eye on those other two. They seem harmless, but you never know."

"He's clean," says Rollins. He pulls a wallet from the back pocket of Mike's jeans.

"Check his ID," she orders.

"Who are you clowns?" Mike says, sneering. "Because you've just made a big mistake."

"The only mistake was yours when you decided to mess with the feds," I say. "And with me. No one leaves a dead body in my dumpster and gets away with it."

"The feds?"

"That's right. The feds as in the Federal Bureau of Investigation. The gig is up, El Tigre."

"Stop calling me that stupid name!" Mike roars.

Agent Rollins clears his throat, "Ma'am?" he says addressing his boss. He holds up Mike's wallet. "According to the driver's license, this man's name is Michael Armandi. There's another piece of ID too. Says he's a member of the Jersey City police force. Homicide Division."

Chapter Eighteen

"IT'S OBVIOUSLY A FAKE ID," I say. "Mike Armandi is El Tigre. He has to be."

Mike shakes his head. "If you call me that one more time—"

Agent Billings puts a hand in the air. "Hold on, everyone." She looks at me. "Fontaine here said you sent him a 911 message. Did this guy," she indicates Mike, "try to hurt you?"

"Hurt me? Well, no not yet."

"Unbelievable," Mike mutters.

"Did he confess to being El Tigre?" she demands to know.

Brittany stomps her foot. "Who is this El Tigre? I insist that someone explain everything at once! I'm a member of the Whispering Bay Chamber of Commerce, and as a representative of the city, I have to say this has all been completely unacceptable."

Agent Billings gives Brittany a look that shuts her up fast. "Check out that ID," she snaps at Rollins. He takes off like a man on a mission.

The door to the kitchen opens again. This time it's Sarah. She takes everything in, including the gun that Agent Billings is still holding on Mike. "Oh my." Her gaze darts between mine and Travis's.

"I can explain." For the first time, I'm beginning to feel uncertain. Homicide Division? No, that ID *has* to be a fake. If Mike was a cop, why didn't he tell me before? Why is he here delivering restaurant supplies and offering to take out people's nasty smelling trash?

Fifteen minutes later, we're all still in the kitchen, waiting. Travis went out to the dining area to inform the customers that no one can leave and that we're on lockdown. I can just imagine how well that's going over.

After what seems like an eternity, Agent Rollins comes through the door. "Armandi's credentials have all checked out."

"Damn right they did." He turns to Agent Billings, his eyes gloating. "Want to put the gun down now?"

She hesitates, then lowers the gun. "What's the deal?" she asks Rollins.

"According to the chief in Jersey City, Armandi is on a paid leave of absence. He spent six months working a case involving a drug-related murder. Says the case really did a number on his head and he was down here in Florida for some R&R." He glances at Mike. "Says you're one of his best, and he expects you back soon."

What? *No.* This can't be right.

I whirl around to face El Tigre ... er, I mean Mike. "But you broke your uncle's leg! You said so yourself!"

"What are you talking about?"

"You said you broke his leg because he got in your way!"

"Yeah, playing football. We were supposed to be playing a friendly game of touch, but I got carried away and I tackled him. I feel awful about it too. Pops was going to take over Rocko's route, but it was a lot of work, so I offered to help."

"Oh. I see." My voice sounds little. I wish I could make the rest of me little too, or better yet disappear. Preferably to Siberia or somewhere else far away.

"So the gun ... yes, yes, it makes sense now. But why did you lie to me about never being near a crime scene?"

"Because I didn't want to get into the whole cop thing. My chief was right. That last case messed me up. I even thought about quitting the force and moving to Florida to open a diner." He does a double take. "Wait. How did you know I lied about never being at a crime scene?"

Everyone turns to look at me.

Oops. I shouldn't have let that slip.

"Um, lucky guess?"

"Who is this El Tigre?" Mike asks. "I think I have a right to know."

"No, you don't. You can go now," says Agent Billings. "Please accept the Bureau's apology for the misunderstanding."

"Yeah, whatever," he says, clearly disgusted.

Agent Rollins hands him back his wallet with a shrug. Mike goes to leave, but before he gets to the door, he turns to look at us. "To think, I actually thought about relocating to this crazy town. No, thanks, give me Jersey City any day."

"I'm so sorry," I rush to say. "Please forgive me. It was just a big misunderstanding."

He looks at me like I'm a bug he could squash but doesn't want to waste the energy. "Next time you get the urge to play detective, go make some cupcakes instead."

Muffins, not cupcakes! I want to say, but I don't think that will go over very well right now.

Travis and Zeke manage to control the guests in the dining room. As far as our customers know, the "super-elite state CSI team" had a breakthrough in the murder of the guy found in our dumpster and they needed everyone to stay put while they checked it out. Now that the situation has been resolved, everyone is free to go. Will and the library crew are the first to leave, but not until he makes me promise to call him as soon as I get a chance.

Everyone else leaves one by one, including mom and dad and all their friends. Mom insists that I come to dinner tonight, and for once, I'm not going to argue. It will be nice to be around people who actually like me, as opposed to everyone who was in the kitchen when I accused Mike of being a mafia hitman. None of whom are very happy with me right now, except Sarah, who is always so supportive and upbeat. And Paco, of course. But he's a dog, and he'd love anyone who fed him, so he doesn't count.

"It's an innocent mistake. It could have happened to anyone," says Sarah, trying her best to console me.

How could I have thought Mike was El Tigre?

I'll never forget the look on his face when he walked out. I should have listened to Will and left this to the professionals instead of always thinking that I know more than anyone.

Since Sarah, Brittany, Tara, and Man Bun were all present in the kitchen when the action went down, they know that the secret elite team is really the FBI. Agent Billings and her crew grilled them on what they saw and made them promise not to tell anyone on penalty of "extreme repercussions." Tara threatened to sue them, but that just made them laugh.

She gathers her things in a huff. "C'mon, Wade, let's get out of here. We're going to Catfish Cove."

"For the last time, it's Wayne! And you can go yourself, you ridiculous cow, because I quit."

The look on Tara's face is almost funny. "You can't quit."

"Sure I can. I just got the call. I'm getting my old job back at the public access channel. You can stick your cable channel where the sun don't shine." He picks up the pieces of his broken camera, then stomps out the door.

Tara takes off after him, and Brittany runs after them both. "Wait! Does this mean Whispering Bay is out of the running for *Battle of the Beach Eats*?"

Brittany comes back a few minutes later looking defeated. "Well, that's that."

"I'm sorry," I say, cringing as I wait for Brittany to blame me for all this.

But instead of chiding me and telling me this is all my fault, she does something worse. She blinks back tears. "Everyone is right. I'm a disaster. The only reason I got the chamber of commerce job is because of Daddy. And now I've let everyone down. I have no idea how I'm going to justify buying all those door wreaths!"

"You're not a disaster," I say. "You've worked your butt off for this town. The chamber of commerce is lucky to have you."

She wipes the tears from her cheeks. "You're only saying that because you're my best friend."

"Well ..." I try to think of something to console her, but I'm not as good at this as Sarah.

Brittany leaves to go back to work and try to salvage her job, and since we've driven away all our customers, Sarah and Jill take off as well. That leaves just me, the cops, and the FBI.

Agent Billings is in the middle of chastising me for jumping to conclusions and creating a lot of trouble. And just when I think that my day couldn't possibly get any worse. It does.

Agent Parks comes up to us with an expression of total and utter fear. He's holding a clear baggie in his hand. "I'm sorry to interrupt, ma'am, but I thought you might want to see this." He holds up the baggie. There's a button inside. "We found this in the parking lot about two feet from the dumpster. We've just verified it's a button from the shirt Rinaldi was wearing when he was murdered."

Agent Billings' gaze sharpens. "El Tigre's signature clue. So today hasn't been a total waste then. Let's get the footage off the camera in the parking lot and see what we're dealing with."

Agent Parks clears his throat. "That's just it, ma'am, I'm afraid someone disabled that camera."

"Disabled it?" The disbelief on her face mirrors my own.

"How did they do that?" I ask.

"Not they," she says tightly. "He. While we were in the kitchen listening to your nonsensical rantings, the real El Tigre was making fools of us all."

"But—"

"C'mon," Agent Billings snaps at her people, "we have less than eight hours to get out of here."

"Where are you going?" I ask.

"To take Joey somewhere safe. Which means as far away from Whispering Bay as possible."

If I thought Mike was disgusted, that was nothing in comparison to the way Agent Billings looks at me. It's like I'm a wad of gross sticky gum stuck beneath her favorite shoe.

"I have no idea how you caught The Angel of Death. You must have bumbled your way into solving that. From now on, McGuffin, do the

United States a favor and stay away from Bureau business before you take the entire country down with you. Got it?"

Chapter Nineteen

I TOLD BRITTANY SHE wasn't a disaster and I was right.

I'm the disaster.

Now that everyone's gone, I'm lying on my living room couch feeling sorry for myself. Paco is snuggled next to me. He gives me a look that's different from all the other looks I've cataloged so far. I've decided to call this the *Don't Cry, Lucy* look because his brown eyes are pleading with me, telling me that it's all going to be okay. Intellectually, I know that's true. I'll live this down eventually. In about another ten years or so.

I thought going to my parents for dinner would be a good idea, but I can't face them just yet, so I call Will and tell him I'm coming over.

He's waiting with a big chocolate bar for me and a bone for Paco. Paco greedily snatches the bone and takes it off into a corner of the living room, but I'm not in the mood for chocolate or anything else. I've never gotten the concept of being too distressed to eat before, but I get it now.

"Are you sick?" Will teases when I turn down the chocolate.

Since he was part of the group in the dining area that's oblivious to what went down in the kitchen, I fill him in on everything. How I accused a Jersey City homicide detective of being a ruthless hitman, and all the while, El Tigre got the best of everyone.

"You told me not to do it, but did I listen? No."

"Sure you don't want that chocolate? I've got whiskey too."

"No, thanks."

"C'mon, Lucy, none of this is your fault."

"Then whose fault is it?"

"The FBI's. They should have never involved you in this. It was unprofessional of them."

"I feel like I let everyone down. Including Brittany. I was hoping we still had a shot at the Cooking Channel show." I shake my head. "I don't know, it's all those lies Mike told. They totally threw me in the wrong direction."

Will studies me a minute. "Have you ever thought that maybe your ability to tell when someone's lying could actually be a hindrance?"

Just all the time.

"What do you mean?" I ask.

"If you didn't know that Mike had lied to you, would you have been so suspicious of him?"

I think about Will's question. To be fair, the answer is probably no.

"You're right. As usual."

"Don't take it so hard. Like I said, this isn't your fault."

I have to admit Will is making me feel just the teeniest bit better.

"So how's work?" I ask, because I don't want this to always be about me.

"Busy. I'm writing up a grant that will hopefully let us update our computer system."

"Sounds boring."

"It is."

"Why don't you get someone else to write the grant? Like Sally. She's pretty sharp, isn't she?"

"Yeah, but she's going on a leave of absence."

"Where to? She just got here."

"Wyoming. Her dad's sick, and she's the only family he's got left."

"That's too bad. I really like her."

"Hopefully she'll be back."

"Maybe we can give her a going away party? I could make muffins."

Will chuckles.

I'm starting to feel hungry, which is a good sign. I check the time. We still have an hour before my parents expect us. "How do you think El Tigre was able to disable those cameras?"

Will moans. "Not again. Lucy, you're like a dog with a bone."

"I know. Sorry, but just hear me out. The feds have been keeping watch since yesterday, but they just now noticed that the camera was disabled. Does that make sense to you? That button was left there sometime today, which means that El Tigre was at The Bistro today." I sit up straight. "El Tigre was at The Bistro today," I repeat slowly.

"Okay," says Will. "He could have come and gone anytime, right? Unless the FBI had agents in the parking lot?"

"Will," I say, getting excited. "There's no way El Tigre could have gotten into the parking lot and disabled that camera on his own. Not without inside help."

"You think one of the FBI agents is crooked?"

"Maybe one of the FBI agents *is* El Tigre." The second I say it out loud I shake my head because instinctively I know it's wrong. "That's not right. I thought maybe Ken Cameron was dirty and that's why he was killed. But think about it. Why would El Tigre kill Ken Cameron so early in the game? Why not wait until after he had no more use for him?"

"You mean after he kills this Weasel person?"

"Exactly."

"El Tigre has killed three people here in Whispering Bay since this whole thing started." I count them off with my fingers. "Ken Cameron in the city park. Mark Rinaldi at The Bistro. And Eddie O'Leary at The Harbor House. But the feds have only been concentrating on The Bistro. According to Agent Billings, El Tigre always leaves a clue. It's like a big *I gotcha* to the feds. Which means there's probably two clues still left to find. One in the city park and one at The Harbor House."

"Maybe the feds already found them."

"I don't think so. They put all their resources into finding the clue at The Bistro. Their main focus is on keeping Joey alive. Catching El Tigre would have just been an added benefit." I jump off the couch. "If we leave right now we'll have time to check out the park before going to my parents for dinner."

Will makes a face. "Do we have to?"

I make a face back.

He sighs. "Okay. I'm driving."

Will leads the way through the city park, shining a flashlight on the grass. It's just after six, but it's already dark. The park lights provide adequate lighting for safety, but unlike a few nights ago when Paco found Ken Cameron's body, the nearby soccer field lights are turned off. "Tell me why we're doing this again?"

"Because it's a loose end and I hate loose ends."

Paco trots between Will and me sniffing at the ground and marking the shrubs along the way. When we get to just a few feet away from the sable palm where we found Ken Cameron, Paco stills, like he remembers.

Will shines his flashlight at the base of the tree. "What are we looking for exactly?"

"I don't know. It could be anything, but it's something El Tigre took off Ken Cameron's body after he killed him."

"Like a trophy?"

"Exactly, except he doesn't keep it to commemorate his kill, he returns it to the scene of the crime to show the feds how much smarter he is than they are."

"Sick bastard."

"I'll say."

Will leans over and picks something up off the ground. "Here's a bottle cap. Probably not what we're looking for, huh?" He tosses it into a nearby trashcan.

The two of us, along with Paco, scour the area going a few feet off in each direction, then make our way back to the base of the tree again. We repeat the pattern until we've checked out the entire radius. Even with the park lights on it's still not optimal. This would be so much easier during the daytime.

"Maybe you're right," I say, "Maybe the feds did come here and find the clue. After all, there's no reason they'd share that with me." I glance at my watch. "We only have about twenty minutes until we're supposed to be at my parents."

"You want to give up?" Will asks.

"Let's give it one more try. If we don't find anything, then I say we call it a night."

We start back at the base of the tree and begin to work our way around the area when Paco sits and starts to stare up the sable palm. "Oh God, not another squirrel."

Will whips around. "Did you say squirrel?"

More than anyone Will knows how I react to the horrible little creatures.

"What are you staring at, boy?" He aims his flashlight at the spot that Paco seems to be concentrating on so hard. "Lucy, I think there's something sticking out of one of the palm boots." Will reaches into the palm boot and pulls out what looks like a piece of white string. He turns it over in his hand. It's a shoelace.

"This is from a running shoe," he says quietly.

There's no way a shoelace ends up tucked inside a palm tree unless someone placed it there on purpose.

I try to visualize Ken's body the way it looked the night Paco and I found him. He was still wearing the same jogging outfit I'd seen him in earlier in the day. "I'd bet you anything Ken Cameron's body went to the morgue missing a shoelace on one of his sneakers."

"Should we call the cops?" Will asks.

"After today? They'd probably hang up on me."

"Travis won't."

Maybe. Maybe not. He was pretty mad at me. Or disappointed. I'm not sure which is worse.

"Pretty clever of El Tigre to hide the clue in the actual tree," Will says.

I shine my flashlight back to the spot where Will pulled out the shoelace. It's just a bit above my head, so I don't have to reach up very high. "Maybe he left something else in there too." I feel around, but there's nothing. Then I spot a brightly colored thread. I ease it out. It's about six inches long and pink.

Will examines it. "Do you think this came from Ken Cameron's clothing?"

"No. He was wearing dark colored jogging pants and a blue hoodie. No pink."

I rub the thread between my fingers. "Will ... this isn't a fiber or any kind of material."

"Was is it then?"

"It's a thread of hair."

Chapter Twenty

MY BRAIN STARTS DOING this weird sorting thing, pushing facts and bits of info all around until everything lines up and makes sense.

Holy wow.

I know who El Tigre is. All this time it was right there in front of me, staring me straight in the face.

Will examines the strand closer. "How did a pink hair get inside a palm boot?"

"It was put there. Alongside the shoestring."

"By El Tigre?"

"She just couldn't help herself. Think, Will. Who do you know that has pink hair? Or at least had pink hair the day of the murder."

Will laughs nervously. "Lucy, you're not suggesting—"

"Sally Reynolds is El Tigre."

Will is quiet for a few seconds. Then he begins to pace around the tree. The pacing is something that I normally do while Will watches on, but I suppose the idea that a notorious hitman ... er, hitwoman, has been under his nose this whole time is a lot to take in.

"I can't believe I'm going to encourage this, but tell me your reasoning here."

"Number one, Sally conveniently came to town just a couple of weeks before Joey and the feds showed up. Where did she come from?"

Will thinks on this a second. "Miami? Yeah, she worked at one of the Dade County library branches."

"I bet her references were excellent."

"They were the best I've ever seen."

"I also bet they're not real."

"She got to town before the whole FBI thing happened," Will says. "Explain that one."

"The feds didn't just hop on a plane and take Joey somewhere random. They had that safe house in place for weeks before they pulled Joey out of the mob. I already told you, El Tigre has to be working with one of the FBI agents. Maybe it's even Billings herself."

"Okay, but that doesn't mean Sally is El Tigre."

"She's familiar with all the body dump sites—The Bistro, the city park, and I imagine she's been to The Harbor House too."

"So has everyone else in Whispering Bay."

"She was at The Bistro today and ... Will, she lied to me. I found her wandering near the pantry. She pretended she was lost like she didn't know where the bathroom was, but that's not true. The hallway near the pantry leads to a back door to the parking lot. It was her opportunity to leave the button out by the dumpster."

"Maybe she just forgot where the bathroom was." Will frowns. "Except ... yeah, I admit, that doesn't sound like Sally."

"She lied to you too."

"When?"

"When she told you that she's the only family her father has left. That's not true. She has a brother."

"How do you know?"

"Because she told me."

"Maybe she was lying when she told you that."

"No, no she wasn't. I know one hundred percent she didn't lie about that. Her brother suffers from sciurophobia, just like me ... and, oh my God. She knows where the safe house is! She was on her way there to kill Joey last night but she ran into me. Will, we have to warn Joey."

"Lucy," he says gravely, "are you sure about this?"

"Will, you have to trust me. I know I'm right this time."

"Do you have the FBI's number?"

"Even if I did have it, I'm not sure who to trust."

"Let's call Travis."

"You call him. He won't believe me, not after the mess I made today, but he might believe you."

Will pulls out his cell phone and punches in the number. After a few seconds, his face falls. "It went to voice mail." He hesitates. "Should I leave a message?"

I nod. "Tell him we know who El Tigre is, and we're on our way to the safe house."

I get Will to park his car a block away from the safe house. "In case someone's looking out the window," I explain. "That way we have the element of surprise on our side."

"I don't like the sound of that."

"You left Travis the message. He's probably already on his way here with reinforcements."

"Let's hope so." Will looks both ways down the street. There's not much activity, but all the houses are lit up, and most either have the front door or porch light on. "You're sure there's just one entrance into the neighborhood?"

"Yep. I checked it out when I was here last night. There's a service road entrance for big truck deliveries, but there's a gate that's locked unless it's being used."

We quietly walk along the sides of the houses until we get to the safe house. The front porch light is on, but all the blinds are drawn and just like before, there's no car parked in the driveway. The garage door is closed. Luckily there's no fence, so we continue to creep along to the backyard until we find some hibiscus bushes to hide behind.

"You think Joey and the feds are still in there?" Will asks, careful to keep his voice low.

"Not sure. They might have been able to get out, but ..." I shrug. "The only way to know for certain is to try to get a peek inside."

"Absolutely no," Will says. "We stay right here till Travis and the cops come."

"I agree." I might be occasionally rash, but I'm not stupid.

Paco starts to whine. "We should have left him in the car," Will says tightly. "What if he starts barking?"

I take Paco's little face into my hands and stare into his eyes. I read somewhere that dogs and humans bond through eye contact. The way he's looking at me is the same way I'm looking at him. I've only had him a few weeks, but I love him already, and I know he loves me. He's saved my life. And even though Will scoffed at the idea of Paco being a ghost whisperer, it's only because he's never seen him in action.

"You have to be quiet, okay?" I say to my little dog. "No barking. No matter what you see. Got it?"

Paco wags his tail, which I take as an enthusiastic yes.

Nothing happens for a few minutes. The sound of a door slamming makes us both jump.

"Where did that come from?" I ask.

"Inside the house, I think. We need to call the cops again. If Travis doesn't answer, then I'm calling Zeke Grant directly." Will pulls out his cell phone and stares at the screen in disbelief. "Crap. There's no service here. We must be in a dead zone. Try yours."

"I left my phone in your car."

He glances around. "I'm going to sneak around to the front of the house and see if I can get cell service. You and Paco stay here."

Before he can take off, I grab his hand. "Will, be careful."

He gives me a reassuring smile. "I'll get the cops here, Lucy. No worries." He vanishes into the darkness.

Paco licks my neck to reassure me. The whole thing is unnerving. What's going on inside the house?

A thudding sound splits through the silence.

I stand up from my crouching position and inch toward a window. I can't see inside because of the closed blinds but I can see the lights are on. There's a tiny sliver of sight that isn't obscured by the blinds. I spy a refrigerator, so I must be right outside the kitchen.

I squint, trying to make out more of the scene. There's a foot. Only the person isn't standing. The position indicates that they're lying down …. Uh-oh. That's not good.

Paco starts to whimper.

Another *thud*.

Chills run down my spine. I'm pretty sure I just heard something big hit the floor. Like a body.

Paco's whimpering becomes louder.

I wrap my arm around his neck to soothe him, but it doesn't work. He turns back to look at me. His eyes have a wild look in them.

Oh no.

I know this look.

Before I can restrain him, he lunges for the door. He's not barking, but he's whimpering so loudly that he might as well be. "Paco!" I hiss, "get back here right now."

I run to grab him when the door opens.

Sally stands in the doorway. She's wearing a black jogging suit and her green hair is tucked beneath a baseball cap. She's also got a gun pointed straight at my head.

Her eyes widen in recognition. "Lucy, I have to say, I'm surprised to find you here."

I try to keep my voice from trembling. "Sally! Do you live here? So sorry to interrupt! We'll just be on our way—"

"Be quiet. You know good and well that I don't live here." She nods toward the kitchen. "Inside. Now."

"Thanks, but Paco and I were going for a walk. We'll just be running along—"

"I'm not going to ask again, Lucy. Get inside. And your little dog too."

Oh no. She's not going to get Paco. No way.

I snatch him up and toss him as far away from me as possible. He lands on his feet. "Run, Paco! Run, boy!" He hesitates for just a second, then he takes off running into the night.

I heave a sigh of relief.

"Off to chase more squirrels, no doubt. Worthless dog," Sally mutters. Then she reaches out with her free hand and pushes me inside the kitchen and slams the door behind us.

The first thing I notice is a couple of my uneaten pumpkin spice muffins on the counter. Uh-oh. Usually those things don't last but a few minutes. I hope I didn't overdo the cinnamon.

The next thing I notice is Agent Parks and Agent Rollins lying on the floor, side-by-side. Dead. With matching bullet holes between their eyes.

Chapter
Twenty-One

SALLY FOLLOWS MY HORRIFIED gaze. "That's right. I'm not quite the mild-mannered librarian I pretend to be."

"You're El Tigre."

"You know about that?" She doesn't bother to hide her surprise. "What gave me away? Wait. Don't tell me. You didn't buy my lost little lamb routine at The Bistro today? Still," she muses, "that's hardly enough to put two and two together."

"You lied to Will about going to Wyoming to take care of your father. You told him you didn't have any other family. What happened to your brother? The one with the sciurophobia?"

"Sciurophobia," she scoffs. "There's no such thing. And I didn't lie to Will. I lied to you. If I did have a brother, he wouldn't have something as pathetic as a fear of squirrels."

"You didn't lie to me about your brother. That whole story about him being in counseling? You were telling the truth."

"Are you sure about that, Lucy?"

The cocky way she looks at me makes me question myself. But only for an instant. I've never been so grateful for my gift before.

"As sure as I'm standing here."

The two of us play a game of chicken staring each other down. After a few long seconds, she grudgingly says, "Okay, so I didn't lie to you about that. I have a brother. So what? Is that it? That's how you figured out I was El Tigre?"

"Not quite. It was a bunch of other little things as well. But what put it all together was the clue you left in the sable palm. The one tucked in along with Ken Cameron's shoestring."

"*No.*" Her voice hitches with excitement. "You actually found it?"

"Yep. A lock of pink hair. You shouldn't have done that. If the FBI had found it instead of me, they'd be running that through the DNA database right now, and you'd be toast."

"It's the first time I've left anything of value behind. I couldn't help myself. Do you know how many kills I've returned to? To leave some worthless trinket? Only to let the feds know that I wasn't just there once, but twice? That I'd outsmarted them once again? We all want to be seen, Lucy, even when we're trying to hide." Her smile gives me the chills. To think, I actually wanted to start a book club with her!

"I'm glad you were the one to find it and not the FBI. Not that my DNA is in their database, but if they analyzed it then they would have found out I was a woman, so, thank you, Lucy. You saved me from myself. Next time El Tigre," she says with mocking emphasis, "will have to control her urges a little better."

"Why do they call you that?"

"Beats me. I suppose someone at the FBI thought it sounded very macho. Of course, the idiots think I'm a man. I'd much rather be called Khaleesi or Xena. What do you think? Fierce warrior princess or ... fierce warrior princess with dragons?"

"You *kill* people. For money. You don't deserve to be called either of those."

She snickers then waves the gun to point me in the direction of the living room. "In there." Since I really don't want to get a bullet between the eyes, I do as I'm told.

Sitting on a chair in the middle of the living room is a skinny middle-aged bald guy with deep-set eyes. So this is the infamous Joey "The Weasel" Frizzone. His hands are tied behind the chair, and his mouth is gagged. "Joey, meet Lucy, Lucy, well … there's no need for introductions because your friendship isn't going to last much longer."

Joey's eyes go wide with fear. He struggles against the ropes but gets nowhere.

I wish I could say something to reassure him, like tell him that the cops are on their way, but if I do that what's to stop Sally from killing us both right now and escaping before they have a chance to storm the place? Plus, there's the fact that Will is somewhere outside, clueless to what's going on in here. Has he found Paco? I hope so.

My best bet right now is to keep Sally talking until the cops arrive.

"Where's Agent Billings?" I ask. "Is she the one who's been helping you?"

"Lucy, I'm impressed. I mean, I knew you were smart, but I had no idea." She checks her watch. "I have a few minutes to answer questions. So, why not? What do you want to know? Oh, you want to know if Billings was helping me. That would be a no. It was the two idiots lying on the kitchen floor."

"Parks and Rollins?"

"Is that their names?" She shrugs. "I just called them Thing One and Thing Two. I never could tell them apart. They were useful, but I have no intention of splitting my contract fee with them. Or anyone else either."

"They were the ones who disabled the surveillance cameras at The Bistro so you could leave Mark Rinaldi's shirt button near the dumpster. That's what you were doing, isn't it, when I caught you in the pantry hallway?"

"That would be a big yes."

"And last night, when I caught you jogging here on the street, you were on your way to kill Joey, weren't you? Parks and Rollins tipped you off on the location of the safe house."

"Not exactly. That would be you, Lucy. You're the one who told me where the safe house was."

"*Me*? I did no such thing!"

"Of course you did. Think back to a few days ago when you came to see Will at the library. You told him all about your adventure following the cops to deliver food to some mysterious jogger? Quite the little sleuth, aren't you? Let's see, what did you say again? A house on a cul-de-sac in Dolphin Isles and the broker who manages the property is named Kitty Pappas. With all that information it only took a few minutes on the Internet to get the address."

"You were eavesdropping?"

"Hardly. The door to Will's office was partially open. I can't help it if my desk is just a few feet away."

The realization that I inadvertently helped El Tigre makes me sick. I'm so angry I could spit on her muffins the next time she comes into The Bistro. Except ... she won't be coming back to The Bistro and I might not be alive to bake any more muffins.

I swallow hard. *Keep her talking, Lucy.*

"So, you killed Mark Rinaldi and Eddie "The Hatchet" because you wanted the money for yourself."

"Money had nothing to do with those hits. That was a matter of keeping order. Once I gave notice that I was in town those two should have backed off. Nobody takes a contract out from under me. It's a good lesson for anyone else who might think to cross me in the future."

"Gave notice?"

"Agent Cameron. He was my notice."

My blood turns cold. "You killed Ken Cameron as a warning? To anyone else who might think to kill Joey?"

"Joey is *my* contract. No one else's. What did you want me to do? Send Rinaldi and O'Leary a Hallmark card telling them their services weren't needed? I'm afraid they don't make greeting cards for that occasion." She giggles at her own joke, then sighs. "Oh, don't sweat it. Agent Cameron didn't suffer. I've worked hard to perfect my skills. One bullet clean between the eyes. You see, I hate making a mess." She points her gun at Joey. "This one, though. He's going to be a challenge."

"What do mean?"

"Vito wants him to suffer. I'm supposed to cut his tongue out before I shoot him as a warning to anyone else who might think of squealing against the Scarlotti family. Preferably with a dull knife, but, I'm just not a knife girl. To tell you the truth, they kind of scare me." Her eyes light up. "Say! You could do it for me."

I almost throw up in my mouth. "*What*?"

She checks her watch again. "We need to get going. I have about five minutes before Billings wakes up, and I'd like to shoot her before then."

"Where is she?"

"In the bathroom, tied up. Thing One did that for me while Thing Two was tying up Joey. I'm going to miss them on my next job. It was nice having help for a change. Oh, well. You should have seen their faces when they realized there wasn't going to be a next job for them."

"You ... you don't have to kill Agent Billings. We won't tell anyone about you. I'll make her promise."

"Don't be such a child, Lucy. Of course, I have to kill her. Not that it will give me any pleasure. I admire her, you know. A woman in her position in the FBI? She's worked hard to get where she is at such a young age. She doesn't deserve to be killed protecting this scum," she says cocking her head at Joey. "The least I can do is kill her before she wakes up. You help me with Joey and I'll do the same for you too. I'll make sure your death is as painless as possible."

"Gee, thanks."

A movement out of the corner of my eye catches my attention. Someone is in the kitchen. Could Parks or Rollins still be alive? No. That would be impossible. Maybe it's the cops. *Keep her talking, Lucy*, I remind myself. It's my only hope to keep everyone alive.

"Let me get this straight," I say. "You want me to cut out Joey's tongue?"

Joey's eyes go even wider than before. He bucks against the chair.

"Sorry but I'm not doing that."

"Too bad." Sally backs up a couple of feet and aims her gun at my face.

"Wait! Hold on! Okay, okay, I'll do it."

She chuckles. "I knew you'd give in." While still keeping the gun on me, she picks a knife up off the coffee table then hands it to me. Why hadn't I noticed it before? I could have grabbed it and ... and what? Stabbed her with it? Not when she has a gun on me. I'm not that fast. Plus, *ew*, it's a knife.

"Just in case you think about trying to be a hero, let me warn you. You come near me with that knife and you'll be dead in two seconds flat. I might not be good with silverware, but I'm an expert when it comes to guns."

My palms are so sweaty that the knife nearly slips out of my grasp. "How do I do this?"

"Just pull his tongue and slice it off. It's easy. I was just joking about the knife being dull."

I walk over to Joey.

Where are the cops?

"Um, he's still gagged. How am I supposed to cut his tongue off if I can't get to it?"

"I guess I have to do everything." Sally pulls the gag off.

Joey immediately starts screaming. "No! Stop! I'll give you anything! You want money? I got money!" He squirms violently, causing the chair to rock from side-to-side. For a minute I think he might topple over. Which might not be such a bad idea. It would distract Sally, that's for sure.

I try to steady the knife. If Joey could just get the chair to tip over then I could—

In that instant, I see more movement in the kitchen. It's Will! And Paco.

Sally has her back to them so she can't see them. Thank God.

Will and I lock gazes. He shakes his head, warning me not to give him away. Paco is by his feet. His eyes have a hard glassy look in them. I've seen this look before. It's his *I have to save Lucy*! look.

It feels as if there's a stick of dynamite ready to go off inside my chest. Sweat drips down my back.

"I don't have all day." Sally waves the gun in my face again, which must be too much for Paco, because before I know it, he runs into the living room and leaps in the air rushing Sally from behind.

The gun falls from her hands and skitters onto the floor. Will scrambles to pick it up, but like Sally warned me—she's fast. She's going to beat Will to the gun.

Unless I do something about it first.

Using one of my childbearing hips, I bump into Joey's chair as hard as I can. He topples over, screaming obscenities all the way down, and lands on top of Sally. Will grabs the gun. The front door crashes open.

"Hands in the air!" yells Travis, brandishing a gun, with Zeke behind him. They're wearing regular clothes. I wish I had a camera right now because the looks on their faces when they see Will holding a gun on Sally is priceless.

"It's about time you got here," Will says. "I left you two messages and finally had to call 911."

Travis catches my gaze. "Sorry. We were in an unmarked car in the back of the neighborhood waiting to escort the FBI and Joey out of town."

Zeke quickly takes in the scene. "What's going on?"

Will still has the gun over Sally's head and the look in his eyes is a little scary, And maybe just a little sexy too. I've always been attracted to Will. I mean, with his dark hair and blue eyes, he's basically Henry Cavil without the cape. But today I saw another side of him. A very manly side that's making me feel warm and tingly all over. "Tell them, Lucy," he urges.

"The long version or the short version?" I ask, bending down to scoop Paco into my arms. "You sweet worthless dog you," I say, giving Sally the stink eye.

Sally sighs heavily. "Never trust the dog," she mutters.

"How about the short version now and the long version later?" suggests Zeke.

"Okay, here goes. Sally Reynolds is El Tigre. She killed Ken Cameron and Mark Rinaldi and Eddie O'Leary. She also killed the two FBI agents in the kitchen—Rollins and Parks, only, they kind of deserved it on account of they were crooked. And Agent Billings—*oh*!"

I run to the bathroom where I find Patricia Billings gagged and tied up on the floor. Her gray eyes blaze with fury.

Zeke, who's followed me into the bathroom, helps untie her.

Agent Billings stands up and rubs her wrists. "You have the situation under control?" she asks Zeke.

"Yes, ma'am," Zeke says. "Or rather, Lucy does."

Her gaze snaps to mine. "Lucy? I heard some of what went on out there." Her expression goes blank. "Rollins and Parks. Where are they?"

"Dead. In the kitchen. Sally ... er, El Tigre killed them. They've been helping her all along."

"I know. So, Ken wasn't dirty after all." There's sadness, but also relief in her voice. She takes a deep breath and looks me in the eye. "On behalf of the Bureau, thank you, Lucy." She puts out her hand.

And because I'm a good sport (and yeah, I really messed up with the whole Mike Armandi thing), I shake her hand.

Agent Billings makes a phone call. Soon the place is swarming with more FBI agents. The first thing they do is whisk Joey out the door. Sally is about to be escorted out too, when she stops and turns around. She looks like she wants to say something but I beat her to it.

"So, all those weeks pretending to be a librarian. Did you really read the books we talked about? Do you even like to read? Or was that all just a big sham?"

"Of course, I like to read. I'm not a total monster."

Well, at least there's that.

"Lucy, don't forget what we talked about before. Life's too short." She tosses me a meaningful look over her shoulder right before the feds take her out of the house in handcuffs.

"What's that about?" Will asks once she's gone.

"Nothing," I say a little too quickly.

He gives me an odd look. That's when I notice he still has the gun in his hand. I'm pretty sure he doesn't realize that he's still holding it. "What now?" he asks Travis.

"We have everything we need from you two," Travis says.

Rats. It's just occurred to me that I missed dinner at my parents. "Will, we have to go. My mom's probably going berserk wondering where I am."

"Yeah, sure." He sounds dazed. Not that I blame him. It's not every day you have a life and death encounter with a notorious killer.

"Let's get out of here," I say, and then because I can't help myself, I add, "Leave the gun, take the muffins."

It's nearly midnight, and I'm still at my parents' house telling the story of how I caught El Tigre for the umpteenth time. Half of Whispering Bay has come and gone to either hear the story, congratulate me, tell me how they thought Sally was suspicious from day one, or eat some of my mother's home-made toffee bars. I definitely have to give that interview to the Whispering Bay Gazette so everyone can read it all at once and I won't have to keep repeating myself.

Mom has barely left the kitchen since all this happened. Her cheeks are flushed as she scurries around the house making sure all our "guests" have had something to eat or drink.

Dad, I think, is stunned by it all.

Paco has had his share of the limelight too. Everyone is praising him and telling me how lucky I am to have him. I couldn't agree with them more.

Will and Travis are both here too, and I have to say it's a bit awkward because:

A. Travis knows how I feel about Will, and he thinks I should tell him.

B. I can't stop thinking about my kiss with Travis.

C. I think I have feelings for Travis too.

It's official. I'm a PG-13 rated ho.

The one upside to all this? Now that everyone in town knows what went down, Betty Jean has come crawling over begging me to join her book club again. Well, maybe not begging, but she's strongly requesting that I consider it.

I told her I'd give her my decision later.

I'll probably say yes, but I plan to make her sweat for a few days.

Sarah and her husband Luke and a bunch of other friends have all come by too. Sarah and I have decided to close The Bistro tomorrow since it doesn't look like I'm going to get to bed any time soon. We'll reopen bright and early Wednesday morning and if anyone has anything to say about that, tough.

My brother is one of the last people to arrive. He hugs me tightly. "Lucy, Lucy, Lucy," he says in his Ricky Ricardo voice that always makes me laugh. Then in a more serious tone, "Are you all right?"

"I'm okay. Thanks to Will and Paco."

He nods thoughtfully in that way he does when he's really thinking about something else.

"What's wrong?" I ask.

He looks startled that I've been able to read him so well.

"Nothing's wrong. Everything's actually pretty right. The bishop called me this afternoon to tell me that someone from the parish is donating all the funds to fix the roof."

"What? That's great, isn't it?"

"Super," he says, "I just wish it wasn't anonymous. I'd like to be able to thank whoever donated the funds."

Mom pulls Sebastian away to ask him a question (I hope she's not asking for the membership roster for the Young Catholic Singles group), so I wander off into the dining room where I find Travis and my dad in deep conversation.

They glance up and Dad takes off, leaving Travis and me alone. I wonder what they were talking about. "Your mom's a great cook," Travis says, pointing to his empty plate.

"She fed you, huh?"

"Yep." He studies me a minute. "Why do I feel like there's something you're not telling me?"

"Like what?"

"What made you suspect Sally in the first place? I mean, the hair, yeah, I get that, but ..." He shakes his head, confused. "What did I miss?"

Poor Travis. I want to tell him about my lie-detecting skills. I really do. I mean, I figure eventually I'm going to have to tell him, but I don't have the energy for it tonight. Maybe on our next adventure. If we have one. Something tells me that we will.

"You didn't miss anything," I assure him.

He opens his mouth to argue with me, when we're interrupted by Brittany.

"Lucy!" She throws herself against me. "Thank God you're alive! When I heard what happened, I nearly fainted. How are you? How's Paco? How's Will? I heard he almost singlehandedly took down this El Tigre person!"

"We're all fine, Brittany, thanks for coming over."

"Of course! Oh, Lucy, you're not going to believe this. I have the best news ever!"

The best news ever according to Brittany would be something in-volving either her job or ... "Don't tell me we're going to be on *Battle of the Beach Eats* after all."

"How did you know?" she squeals.

"Wait. I was ... are you serious?"

"We're back on top! Isn't it fantastic? Tara called me this evening with the news. Wait for it," she says dramatically. "Catfish Cove had a main pipe burst making their tap water undrinkable. *Yes!*" She pumps her fist in the air.

"But, that's horrible."

"Not for us it isn't. All the restaurants there had to close on account of their water problem, so Tara had no choice but to go with us. How lucky are we, huh?"

"Um, well, yeah, but those poor people in Catfish Cove."

She taps her watch. "I'd love to stay but I need to get my beauty sleep." She checks out my face. "You should too, Lucy. You know what they say about the camera! It picks up everything. You don't want to have bags under your eyes, do you?"

"What do you mean?"

"Filming starts at precisely seven a.m. tomorrow morning. I've promised the Cooking Channel people complete access to everything in town."

"Tomorrow? But ... that's like today already. Sarah and I were going to take the day off."

"Day off?" Brittany laughs like I've just said something hilarious. "See you bright and early! Oh, and I left a wreath with your mother. Don't forget to hang it on The Bistro door. You don't want to be the only place in town without one!" She throws me an air kiss on her way out.

I slump down in my chair. In exactly four hours I'll need to start making the muffins. And since it doesn't look as if I'll be leaving here anytime soon, it stands to reason I probably won't get any sleep, which means I'll have bags under my eyes on national TV.

Figures.

THE END

Books By Maggie March

Lucy McGuffin, Psychic Amateur Detective series

Beach Blanket Homicide

Whack The Mole

Murder By Muffin

Stranger Danger

Two Seances and a Funeral

The Great Diamond Caper

Dead and Deader

Castaway Corpse

My Big Fat Cursed Wedding

Honeymoon Homicide Hijinks (coming soon!)

Want to know when I have a new book out? Subscribe to my newsletter at www.maggiemarch.com

About Maggie

Maggie March writes page-turning cozy mysteries filled with humor, unexpected twists, and a little dash of romance. Born in Cuba, she was raised on Florida's space coast, and spent three decades as a labor and delivery nurse before pursuing her passion for writing full-time. She and her husband of thirty-seven years and their 2 little dogs live in central Florida, where she enjoys the beach, going out to lunch with friends, and solving challenging crossword puzzles. She's also on a lifelong quest to discover the ultimate key lime pie recipe (but not the kind they served on Dexter!). With three grown children and an adorable granddaughter, Maggie knows there is nothing better than spending quality time with loved ones.

Maggie loves hearing from her readers. You can write to her at maggie@maggiemarch.com

Maggie also writes heart-warming small-town contemporary romance as her alter ego Maria Geraci.

Acknowledgments

Most of all, I'd like to thank my readers. Without you, there would be no Lucy McGuffin or any of the other zany characters who live inside my head. Thank you for allowing me to pursue my wildest dreams as a published author!

I'd like to thank my copyeditor, fellow author, and friend—Chris Kridler, who tries to keep all my commas straight. Any errors, typos, or other miscellaneous literary no-no's are strictly on me.

Thank you to Kim Killion for my fun covers.

And last but not least, to my better half, my sweet hubby of over 35 years, who always believed in me even when I didn't believe in myself.

Made in the USA
Middletown, DE
21 August 2023

37111551R00111